A Syd...

Welcome t...

Harper, Ivy, Alin... ...the top at Sydney C...... Along the way, they've weathered the highs and lows of life, but one thing has always remained steadfast: their friendship!

Now life's about to take an unexpected turn for the friends—it seems that Cupid has checked in to Sydney Central Hospital!

Come and experience the rush of falling in love as these four feisty heroines meet their matches…

Harper and the Single Dad by Amy Andrews

Ivy's Fling with the Surgeon by Louisa George

Ali and the Rebel Doc by Emily Forbes

Phoebe's Baby Bombshell by JC Harroway

All available now!

Dear Reader,

Thank you for picking up my book, which is the third in the A Sydney Central Reunion series. I always enjoy the chance to collaborate with other authors. After the last two years, when I sometimes felt we were stuck in a time warp and things like travel, meeting new people and getting together face-to-face seemed like distant memories, it was so lovely to be part of this continuity.

Whether you need an escape or just a reason to put your feet up and sit quietly and read, I hope this book, and the other three books in the series, gives you that opportunity.

As always, happy reading.

I'd love to hear from you if you've enjoyed this story or any of my others. You can visit my website, emily-forbesauthor.com, or drop me a line at emilyforbes@internode.on.net.

Emily

ALI AND THE REBEL DOC

—

EMILY FORBES

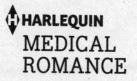

HARLEQUIN
MEDICAL
ROMANCE

Special thanks and acknowledgment are given to Emily Forbes
for her contribution to A Sydney Central Reunion miniseries.

HARLEQUIN®
MEDICAL
ROMANCE™

Recycling programs
for this product may
not exist in your area.

ISBN-13: 978-1-335-59486-0

Ali and the Rebel Doc

Copyright © 2023 by Harlequin Enterprises ULC

For questions and comments about the quality of this book,
please contact us at CustomerService@Harlequin.com.

Harlequin Enterprises ULC
22 Adelaide St. West, 41st Floor
Toronto, Ontario M5H 4E3, Canada
www.Harlequin.com

Printed in U.S.A.

Emily Forbes is an award-winning author of Medical Romance novels for Harlequin. She has written over thirty-five books and has twice been a finalist in the Australian Romantic Book of the Year Award, which she won in 2013 for her novel *Sydney Harbor Hospital: Bella's Wishlist*. You can get in touch with Emily at emilyforbes@internode.on.net, or visit her website at emily-forbesauthor.com.

Books by Emily Forbes

Harlequin Medical Romance

Bondi Beach Medics

Rescuing the Paramedic's Heart
A Gift to Change His Life
The Perfect Mother for His Son
Marriage Reunion in the ER

London Hospital Midwives

Reunited by Their Secret Daughter

Rescued by the Single Dad
Taming Her Hollywood Playboy
The Army Doc's Secret Princess

Visit the Author Profile page
at Harlequin.com for more titles.

Praise for
Emily Forbes

"Ms. Forbes has delivered a delightful read in this book where emotions run high because of everything this couple go through on their journey to happy ever after...and where the chemistry between this couple was strong; the romance was delightful and had me loving these two together."
—*Harlequin Junkie* on *Rescued by the Single Dad*

CHAPTER ONE

'IF ONE MORE auntie asks me when I'm going to settle down, I'm going to scream,' Ali said as she walked into her sister-in-law's kitchen. Dee was bent over a kitchen drawer, her back to Ali as she rummaged through the contents, but Ali kept talking. 'You'd think they'd have given up by now. How many different ways can I say I don't want kids?'

Dee straightened up, a triumphant look on her face as she grasped two candles, both shaped as the number one, in her hand. 'But you're so good with them,' she replied with a grin as she pressed the candles into the centres of two separate cakes.

'Because I can hand them back.' Honestly, Ali couldn't imagine anything worse than having to deal with children twenty-four-seven. That was not her idea of fun. She loved her family, which was fortunate because with four siblings, parents, grandmothers and aunts, uncles and cousins, plus nieces and nephews, there was literally no way of escaping them. Life was a constant stream of family gatherings. Which was why she was amazed that the message hadn't got through. She didn't want to have kids. She didn't plan on having kids.

She loved her nieces and nephews, all ten of them—soon to be eleven—and she loved being Awesome Auntie Li-Li but she didn't want her own children. She never had and she wasn't about to change her mind at this point in her life. When she and Adam had got married, she knew people thought she'd change her tune but that hadn't happened. She also knew people found it hard to reconcile her position with her career as an obstetrician, but she was weary of having to constantly explain her decision. After all, it was her body, her life and her prerogative.

'I hear you,' Dee said with a laugh, 'but I'm not letting you hide in here. Go outside and mingle with my friends.'

'I've delivered most of their babies—I know far more about them than I want to,' Ali said, only half joking. 'I don't need to mingle.'

'Well, in that case, you might as well make yourself useful. Can you take some more plates and forks outside?' Dee passed Ali a stack of bamboo plates. 'I'll bring the cakes out when I find the matches. The sooner we sing "Happy Birthday" the sooner everyone will go home.'

'I thought you liked hosting parties.'

'I do,' Dee said as she let out a big sigh, 'but I'd forgotten that first birthday parties aren't really for the kids but for the adults. I've been going non-stop for two days getting ready, plus today and tomorrow for what? Kai and Leni aren't going to remember this. Remind me not to do this again for the next one.'

'Next one! Are you pregnant?'

'No, I was speaking hypothetically. Perhaps remind me not to get pregnant again as well. Having three kids under three is exhausting.'

'And people wonder why I don't want my own,' Ali said as she grabbed a handful of forks and headed into the garden.

To her left she spied her twin brother standing with his arms wrapped around his fiancée, looking determined not to let her go again. They looked happy and she was pleased for him, she knew their road to happiness hadn't been easy. *Life* wasn't easy.

Yarran was a single dad, raising his son,

Jarrah, on his own since the death of his first wife, and Ali knew that having him finding happiness again at the age of forty had likely reignited the family's idea that it wasn't too late for her to find someone after her marriage break-up.

But, post-divorce, if anyone had asked her the other big question, 'Do you have a man in your life?', she had responded by saying she didn't want one. That she wasn't ready. Adam, her ex-husband, had done a number on her confidence. She had loved the life they'd built together, only to find out it was all a lie, and their break-up had made her wary of relationships. She'd only recently started to, very tentatively, dip her toe in the dating pool again.

She wasn't lonely—but she didn't want to be alone. There was a difference.

Testing the water had meant putting some parameters in place for dating. He would need to be fit, intelligent and older than her, with adult kids or, better yet, no kids. She didn't want to take on anyone else's children, nor did she want to date someone who might eventually want a family. That wasn't something she could offer. At the age of forty, even if she'd wanted kids, which she didn't, as an obstetrician and gynaecologist she knew her chances of conceiving were greatly diminished.

Maybe there was someone out there for her, but if she did happen to meet someone who would make her consider another relationship, she knew it wouldn't ever lead to motherhood. That was not for her.

So, while she was single, she was trying to focus on the positives in her life. Work was her passion. Her focus. Followed by her family. And her close-knit group of friends. She had her career, her health, her family and friends, her own apartment. She had everything she needed.

Except good sex.

That was one thing she'd had with Adam, until he started cheating on her. Her patients had always told her that it wasn't marriage that took the gloss off sex but having kids. That had been another good reason to remain childless, Ali had thought, except now she had neither—she didn't have kids and she wasn't having sex.

Maybe it was time that she did something about that, she mused as Dee brought out the cakes.

Everyone gathered around the table to sing before the twins tried to blow out their candles, eventually needing help from their older sister.

Ali's phone buzzed in her pocket as she handed plates of chocolate cake around. She pulled it out and saw the hospital's number on the screen. As she swiped to answer she was hoping someone needed her. It would give her an excuse to leave and avoid more questions about her personal life.

'Dr Edwards? This is Sylvia, an RN on the general surgery ward. I'm sorry to interrupt your weekend but there's a note here saying to contact you if there are any medical issues regarding Emma Wilson.'

Honestly, why couldn't people just get to the point? she thought. As Head of Obstetrics and Gynaecology, Ali wasn't familiar with the nursing staff on General but she curbed her impatience. Having her weekend interrupted was par for the course, she was well used to it by now and Sylvia was only doing her job.

'What's happening?' Ali asked. She wouldn't normally have patients on this ward, but Emma was complicated. She'd initially been admitted with injuries sustained in a fire, but she also happened to be thirty-two weeks pregnant and was, therefore, now under Ali's care too.

'Her blood pressure is very high. It's one-sixty over one hundred and five. I've checked it a couple of times just now and it's not changing. This morning it was one-thirty over ninety. I thought you should know.'

As far as Ali was aware Emma hadn't had hypertension during her pregnancy but she wasn't surprised to hear her blood pressure was elevated. Emma had undergone multiple surgeries since being admitted to Sydney Central several weeks ago—undergoing skin grafts and then an emergency appendectomy—but that reading was dangerously high and Ali was concerned.

Gestational hypertension wasn't uncommon, but Ali knew that prior to her accident Emma hadn't had any of the usual risk factors and that set alarm bells ringing. Hypertension could be perilous, especially in pregnancy as it could develop into preeclampsia, which could threaten not only Emma's life but the lives of her unborn twins. Ali needed to get to the bottom of this.

'Does she have any other symptoms? Fever? Oedema? Pain?'

'She's afebrile.' That was good, it reduced the likelihood of an infection. 'But she was asking for pain relief, that's when I checked her blood pressure.'

'Where was her pain? Was it a headache? Abdominal pain?'

'Abdominal.'

'Has one of the doctors on duty seen her?'

'It's the weekend so we've only got a registrar. They asked me to call you but I can call Dr Hurst if you prefer?'

Abdominal pain could be attributed to many things, including Emma's previous injuries and surgeries, but Ali's sixth sense was stirring. On numerous occasions she'd sensed things that she couldn't explain—it was something that seemed to run through the women in her family—and over time Ali had learned to trust her instincts. And her instincts were telling her it was related to Emma's pregnancy.

'I'll come in now,' she said. 'If I need to, I can call Dr Hurst once I've seen Emma.' Ivy Hurst was Head of General Surgery and one of Ali's closest friends, she'd definitely consult her if she needed to, but Ali was now Emma's primary medical expert and she wanted to examine Emma. 'Did Emma mention any nausea or visual disturbances?' she queried.

'She didn't mention anything. Would you like me to check?'

'No, that's okay, I'm on my way. Can you

do a urinalysis for protein and a blood test to check liver function? And alert the radiology department; ask them to bring a portable ultrasound down for me and find out who the sonographer on duty is in case I need them.'

Ali needed to be at the hospital. She could wait for the test results to come in, but test results could only tell her so much, and seeing Emma in person would give her information that the numbers couldn't. It also gave her a legitimate excuse to say her goodbyes. She loved her family, but she'd had enough questions for one day.

Ali ran through Emma's history in her head while she drove, knowing she'd familiarise herself with her file when she got to the hospital, but mulling over what she remembered to date.

Emma had been brought to the ED at Sydney Central two months ago. She'd been injured in a house fire, sustaining serious burns to her lower limbs, and Ali's twin, Yarran, had been one of the firefighters who had been involved in her rescue. Emma had undergone skin grafts and then battled infections before also undergoing an emergency appendectomy. To complicate matters further, Emma had been twenty-four weeks pregnant at the time of the accident. To say she'd had a traumatic few weeks was something of an understatement.

Emma had come through the surgeries but remained in hospital waiting for the birth of her babies. She didn't need any further complications. But, luckily Emma was a fighter. Ali just hoped she had some reserves left.

Emma was being managed by a team of specialists that had included Ali from day one because of her pregnancy. As the department head, Ali didn't have a patient caseload as such, but she would give advice or lend her expertise as needed. Emma was a patient who warranted close attention for several reasons, including the fact that she was a high-profile patient as well as high risk.

Emma's husband, Aaron Wilson, was a local celebrity, hosting a top-rated reality television show, and the media interest in Emma's case was enormous because of who she was married to. Emma and Aaron were regulars on the red carpet and in the Sydney society pages. Aaron was a quintessential Aussie man who'd done well for himself. He'd started with nothing except a trade as a carpenter before applying for a spot on a home improvement show and eventually, when the network realised how much the viewers loved him, he'd been offered his own show.

Aaron and Emma were a lovely couple but the intense interest from the media had been another reason Ali had wanted to make sure she was the Ob-Gyn looking after Emma. She wanted to make sure she received the best care, but she also wanted to avoid any negative publicity. It was her responsibility to protect the hospital and her department from that. Ali was new in her role as Head of Obstetrics and Gynaecology and she couldn't afford to have any mistakes. There was enough to deal with in this role as a female and she was determined to prove she'd been appointed to the role on her merits.

It was something she was used to as she was always trying to prove herself. Always making sure no one could question her position. As an Indigenous female she often felt, rightly or wrongly, that she had to work doubly hard—even triply hard—to make sure no one could question her appointment to the top job. Throughout her school and university years she'd strived to be the best, craving recognition of her hard work and intelligence and not wanting to give people an opportunity to cut her down or to say she had been given a hand up the ladder because she was female and Indigenous. She wanted to earn her position and she wanted people to *recognise* that it had been earned. Not given. Not handed to her to meet a quota.

She knew she was doing a good job so far and she had no intention of letting things slip, she thought as she grabbed her stethoscope from her office and headed for the surgical ward.

'Hello, Emma,' Ali greeted her patient. Since Emma's initial admission Ali had only seen her on a handful of occasions for routine pregnancy checks. She had monitored Emma and the babies to ensure they weren't being stressed by Emma's injuries and surgeries. So far, perhaps surprisingly, the babies had been unaffected, but Ali was concerned that might all be about to change.

Today's visit was not routine so she modulated her tone, not wanting to frighten Emma or her husband Aaron, who was sitting beside her. 'How are you doing?'

'I didn't realise they'd called you in on a Sunday, Dr Edwards,' Emma apologised. 'I feel okay, especially compared to what I've been through over the past couple of months. I'm sure this is nothing. Just a blip.'

'How's your pain?'

'Easier.'

Sylvia had accompanied Ali into the room. The blood-pressure cuff was still around Emma's arm and Sylvia inflated it. Ali glanced at the screen, checking the numbers. The reading hadn't changed. It was still higher than Ali would like.

'That's good but now that I'm here there are a few things I want to check, just to be sure.'

She glanced surreptitiously at Emma's fingers, checking for oedema, pleased to note there was no obvious swelling at this stage. She knew there was no point checking Emma's feet as her injuries from the fire would complicate things there.

An ultrasound machine had been wheeled in and left in the corner of the room. Ali pulled the curtain around Emma's bed for additional privacy as she said, 'I'm just going to check the babies.' Ali lifted Emma's pyjama top and squirted gel onto her abdomen ready for the ultrasound. She'd have a quick look and if she saw anything untoward, she'd call a sonographer for a more thorough scan. Blood flow to the babies seemed normal and both babies' heart rates were within a normal range.

'Is everything okay?'

'The babies are fine,' Ali replied. 'Tough, like their mum.'

Emma breathed out a sigh of relief and said to Aaron, 'You can stop squeezing so hard now.'

'Sorry,' Aaron replied, letting go of Emma's hand.

There was a knock on the door and as Sylvia drew back the curtain a second nurse stepped into the room.

'I have the test results,' she said as she handed printouts to Ali.

Ali scanned the list of numbers, absorbing the results. Emma's liver function was within normal limits but there were high levels of protein in Emma's urine, indicating that her kidneys were not working effectively.

'What do they say?' Emma asked.

'Your liver is fine but there are traces of protein in your urine.'

'What does that mean?'

'It means your kidneys are under stress.' It could also be indicative of kidney damage, but Ali hoped that wasn't the case.

'What caused that? What do I do now?'

'There's nothing you can do. You've developed a condition called pre-eclampsia, but it wasn't caused by anything you did,' Ali hurried to reassure her patient. 'It's a complication of pregnancy.'

'Is it related to the fire? To Emma's other injuries?' Aaron asked.

'No.' Ali shook her head. She wasn't a hundred per cent sure that it wasn't related to Emma's recent medical history, but she'd never had a pregnant patient like Emma before, with critical injuries and multiple interventions, so she couldn't rule it out completely. But telling them that wouldn't achieve anything. It didn't really matter how this condition eventuated. What mattered was what happened next.

'There are a few risk factors, most of which don't apply to Emma,' Ali said.

'But there are some that do?' Aaron asked, picking up on what Ali hadn't said.

Ali nodded. 'Yes. We see a higher incidence with first pregnancies and twin or triplet pregnancies but plenty of women have the same risk factors without developing this condition,' she explained, knowing it was crucial to give the right amount of information. Too little would leave them worried. Too much would leave them overwhelmed and anxious. 'Pregnant women with diabetes or who are overweight or used assisted reproductive technologies or have a family history can also be at risk, but Emma doesn't tick those boxes.'

'Does it hurt the babies?'

That was a difficult question to answer. While the babies were in utero they should be fine, but it was almost always impossible to leave them there without risks to both Emma and the babies. 'Not as such,' Ali answered vaguely.

'How do we fix this? What can you give her?' Aaron asked.

'Nothing.' That was the big problem.

'What do you mean nothing? There has to be something you can do?'

Ali knew that some studies suggested that magnesium supplements could help but those same studies also showed that once the urinalysis showed traces of protein it was too late. 'The only cure is to deliver the babies,' Ali told them. Delivering the baby usually dropped the mother's blood pressure pretty quickly.

Aaron and Emma spoke in unison.

'But Emma's only thirty-two weeks.'

'The babies are too small, they can't be born now.'

'I know you're concerned,' Ali replied. Emma was right—the babies would be small, and, because she was carrying twins, they were likely to be smaller than a singleton, but she was wrong to think they couldn't be born now. It wasn't ideal but if Emma's condition worsened the alternative was far worse than premature babies. Both Emma and the babies' lives could be at risk. 'The babies will be small but ninety-five per cent of babies born at thirty-two weeks survive.' In Ali's opinion those odds were good. 'But there is a risk,' she continued, 'a couple actually. The biggest issue for the babies is that their lungs aren't fully developed yet. I can administer corticosteroid injections, which is an anti-inflammatory medicine that helps the babies' lungs to mature. Waiting gives me a chance to do that.'

'You're going to inject the babies?' Aaron asked.

'No, not the babies. I give the injections to Emma but ideally you need two injections, twenty-four hours apart. Which is why I'd prefer to wait if we can.'

'Is it safe to wait?'

'At the moment, yes, but if that changes, I will deliver the babies if it becomes necessary. The other risk is to you, Emma. If your condition worsens it can cause seizures and, in the worst-case scenario, it can be fatal.'

'Emma could die?' Aaron exclaimed.

'That outcome is very rare and usually occurs when the condition hasn't been picked up, but we would be monitoring Emma for any exacerbation of symptoms.'

'So, it's a catch-22? The babies or Emma?'

'No, we're not having to choose. Let me tell you what I recommend. If you agree, I'll organise the first injection for Emma now and hopefully we can delay needing to deliver the babies until you've had both doses. I'll postpone delivering the twins for as long as possible but if we can gain another twenty-four hours that gives them a better chance at having reduced breathing difficulties. You'll be closely monitored and if you develop any additional symptoms, I'll review your situation.'

'What other symptoms are we looking for?' Aaron asked.

'Swelling in Emma's hands, feet or face. Headaches. Visual disturbances.'

'Like what?' Emma asked.

'Black spots. Blurred vision. We'll watch you but you need to report anything unusual, anything you're not sure about, any changes to how you're feeling. I know this sounds scary and it's unexpected and worrying but you're in the best place. We'll keep a close eye on you. Now, would you like me to organise the first injection?'

Emma and Aaron agreed as Ali knew they would.

'You're sure this is the only way?' Aaron asked as he followed Ali out of the room.

'I think this is the best option.' Ali tried to sound calm and in control. She'd made it difficult for them to make any other decision but she was convinced this was the best choice for this situation although the outcome was out of her hands really—all she could do was monitor Emma and hope she had made the right call.

'I feel so useless,' Aaron said. 'It's my job to keep my family safe, to fix things. How did we get here?'

'Aaron, it's *my* job to keep Emma and the babies safe.'

Aaron sighed and Ali stopped walking, wanting to let him finish and then get back to his wife. 'I'm not used to feeling so helpless or inadequate. You know I was a carpenter by trade, back before I got my television gig? Give me some tools and I will fix anything. But I can't fix this. Do you know how useless that makes me feel?'

'Your job is just to support Emma. She is in the best place. I'll take care of her. If I think she's in any danger, I promise I'll intervene, but if I can keep the babies in for just one more day and give the steroids time to work their magic that's one less thing to worry about.' She put one hand on his arm, trying to reassure him, trying to persuade him to return to his wife's bedside. 'I'll be back with the injection.'

Ali sat at her desk and reached for her phone. She'd administered the cortisone injection and spoken to the paediatrician on call. She'd also spoken to Ivy, her good friend and Head of General Surgery, updating her on Emma's condition and checking that Ivy didn't have any other concerns. Ali had wanted a second opinion on the test results and she'd also wanted to ask Ivy how she thought Emma would cope with more abdominal surgery, assuming she'd have to undergo a caesarean section, so soon after her appendectomy. That surgery had been performed through a laparoscope so, in theory, a C-section shouldn't present any problems as long as there was no infection.

Ivy had been more concerned about the need for another anaesthetic so now, on Ivy's recommendation, Ali was making a third phone call, this time to Jake Ryan, the anaesthetist who had looked after Emma during her other surgeries. Ali hadn't met Jake, but Ivy spoke highly of him and so she also wanted to line him up for the procedure if necessary. In her mind there were a lot of benefits to keeping the anaesthetist consistent and she wanted to have all her ducks in a row if Emma needed a third anaesthetic in the space of a few weeks.

It was only when her call went to his voicemail that she remembered it was Sunday. A quick check of the time told her it was after six. Most people, even doctors unless they were on night duty, would have left the hospital.

She left a message asking him to call her mobile when he had a minute before she turned her attention to Emma's file. She updated the notes and then read through the file again, familiarising herself with all the details, wanting to make sure she didn't miss anything. She took her time. She had nowhere else to be.

Ali was in a world of her own, focused on Emma's history, when a knock on her door startled her out of her headspace.

Her door was ajar and she looked up to find a man in green scrubs standing before her.

A stranger.

A tall, handsome stranger.

'Can I help you?' she asked.

'Dr Edwards?' She saw him double-check the nameplate on her office door. 'I'm Jake Ryan, the anaesthetist.'

You're Jake Ryan?

She almost spoke aloud but held her tongue just in time, realising she'd sound rude, but he wasn't what she'd been expecting, not at all.

She took in his features. He had a symmetrical face, fine boned but with a strong jaw and an aquiline nose. His cheekbones were sharp and well defined, chiselled—she didn't know if that was a thing but it was the only way to describe them. His eyes were dark, his lips full and his dark brown hair was thick, cut shorter on the sides but with length on top. At a guess he looked to be in his mid-thirties, over six feet tall, slim and rangy.

'You left me a message,' he said when she remained mute. She hadn't expected an anaesthetist who looked like a menswear model, nor had she expected him to turn up at her door and his appearance had taken her by surprise, leaving her speechless. 'You wanted to talk to me?' he continued. 'About Emma Wilson?'

CHAPTER TWO

'I DID.' Ali finally found her voice and was relieved she sounded normal. She'd half expected her voice to squeak.

'Is now a good time?' he asked as he looked around her office. 'I can come back.'

She shook her head. 'Now is fine.' He obviously got the impression he was interrupting but that was far from the truth. 'I wasn't expecting you to call past,' she said. 'I thought you'd phone me back.'

He shrugged, drawing her attention to his broad shoulders under the thin cotton of his scrubs. He might be lean and rangy, but he was perfectly proportioned with wide shoulders, narrow hips and long legs.

'I was in the hospital,' he explained. 'I saw you'd called me from your office number so I thought I might as well see if you were still in the building.'

He was still standing in her doorway and she realised she hadn't asked him in.

'Come in,' she invited as she stood up and extended her hand. 'I'm Alinta, but please, call me Ali.'

He crossed the room in a couple of long strides and reached for her hand. 'Nice to meet you,' he said as his fingers closed around hers. His grip was firm but not overpowering, strong but not domineering. A standard handshake, nothing out of the ordinary, but his fingers were warm and her skin sparked under his touch. The little burst of heat left her off balance and she almost reached for her desk with her left hand, looking for some support, looking for something to stabilise her.

His touch had disturbed her, not in a bad way, but it left her disconcerted. She knew some would say her equilibrium had been knocked off-kilter, others would say something about her soul but she felt it even more deeply than that. Her ancestors would say his touch had stirred her spirit.

It wasn't an unpleasant feeling but it was unsettling. Unexpected.

She had a flash of recognition as he continued to hold her hand in his. There was something familiar about him but she couldn't put her finger on it. She knew she hadn't met him before, not in this lifetime, but her sixth sense was tingling.

There was an idea of something more substantial, something important, but she couldn't grab hold of it. It was just a fleeting feeling, dancing around the periphery of her brain, refusing to settle. She wanted the thought to settle but she knew she needed to be calm in order for it to make sense and she was far from calm. She was flustered. It was unlike her, but something about Jake was mixing her up.

'You said you wanted to talk to me about Emma?' he asked as she tried one last time to make sense of what she was feeling. But his voice interrupted the sensations that had been swirling around her and they disappeared as quickly as they had arrived when he let go of her hand. 'Has something happened?'

Jake's questions helped her to get back on track.

She gathered her thoughts. 'You know she's pregnant?' she asked, cringing inwardly at the silly comment. Of course he'd know Emma was pregnant. Perhaps her mind wasn't totally focused.

'Yes, of course. She's expecting twins,' Jake replied as they both sat down.

Ali nodded. 'Unfortunately, she's developed pre-eclampsia. She's at thirty-two weeks' gestation now and I'm preparing for the possibility that I may have to deliver her babies early.'

'How early?'

'I don't know yet. I'm hoping to delay as long as possible. I've given her a dose of corticosteroids and I've got my fingers crossed that things might stabilise but I'm not that hopeful, if I'm honest. It's really wishful thinking on my part rather than a feeling based on anything concrete. If I do have to deliver the twins early, Emma will need a C-section and, given her recent trauma, I'd like the delivery of her babies to be as pleasant an experience as possible so I'm planning on performing the C-section with a spinal block so, all going well, she can hold her babies when they're delivered. I'd like you to be the anaesthetist for the delivery—I think that consistency will simplify things and will help Emma feel secure but I wasn't sure if you had an area of speciality anaesthesiology. I needed to know two things—one, are you happy to work in obstetrics and two, can you do a spinal block for Emma?'

'I can do whatever you need. A spinal block shouldn't be a problem. If it's an emergency—and I imagine it could be depending on what happens—she can have another general. She's had a couple, but she didn't have any problems with the actual anaesthetic and it's a few weeks now since her last surgery.'

'That's good to hear.' Ali smiled, finally able to relax. 'I'm hoping we won't have an emergency situation. Emma has had enough to deal with.'

'I agree. So, I'm happy to help in whatever way you need.' He smiled in return as he stood up. 'You have my number. I'll expect a call.'

Was he flirting with her? Ali couldn't tell. She was out of practice as dates had been few and far between lately and her job wasn't particularly conducive to meeting eligible men. Perhaps he was just being friendly.

She watched him as he turned and walked out of her office. He was long and lean. He looked like an athlete. Maybe a long-distance runner. He moved easily. Smoothly. Sensuously.

Ali was unsettled. She shook her head, trying to clear her mind, trying to focus, but all she could think about were his eyes. There was something in them that connected to something in her. His gaze had been intense, his eyes piercing. It almost felt as if he could see inside her head, could read her thoughts. She really hoped that wasn't true. Because her jumbled, chaotic thoughts about him weren't for public consumption.

Jake stepped into the lift. On autopilot he pushed the button to take him from the fourth floor back to the first and as the doors slid closed his thoughts went to Dr Edwards. Ali.

She looked younger than he'd expected. He'd double-checked her office door when he'd seen her, making sure he was in the right place. But the nameplate had read *Dr Alinta Edwards, Head of Obstetrics and Gynaecology*. It had to be her, sitting behind the desk, but she didn't look much older than some of the resident doctors, far too young to be the head of a department.

He was relatively new to Sydney Central. Born and raised in Sydney, he'd studied medicine there but hadn't come across Ali at university. She must be younger than he was, early thirties maybe?

He'd been living in Melbourne and had only recently moved back to Sydney. Roster-wise, he'd got the short end of the stick, covering emergency surgery with lots of weekends and after hours, so it was no surprise he hadn't come across Ali in the hospital either. He'd been called in for a few emergency deliveries, but those had all been handled by other obstetricians. He suspected, as she was Head of Obstetrics and Gynaecology, that Ali's patient caseload would be light and wouldn't routinely include emergencies.

Was it wrong to hope she'd need to call him for Emma?

He didn't want Emma to have more emergency surgery but if it was going to give him a reason to see Ali again it wasn't all bad. She intrigued him. Young. Attractive. No wedding ring. She'd had a serious air about her but when she smiled she was an absolute knockout. With her black hair, brown skin and dark eyes, the flash of white teeth in a wide smile had felt like a powerful punch to the chest, figuratively knocking the air from him.

He hadn't felt such a sudden, unexpected attraction to a woman in a long time and he was keen to see her again.

He checked his watch. He was running late to meet friends for dinner but they would be surprised if he was on time. That was one good thing about his job, no one expected him to be on time and no one would ask why he was late. They'd assume he'd been held up at work, which was mostly true. They wouldn't assume he'd just met someone who had piqued his interest. Who he was keen to find out more about. Will and Chris would be like dogs with a bone if he let that slip.

He hoped she was single. Though it would be just his luck to find out she was very much part of a couple and chose not to wear a ring. But before he could think about dating, he needed to get himself sorted. First up? Finding somewhere permanent to live because staying in his cousin's spare room was not a long-term option.

He'd keep this encounter to himself for now. His love life had been dissected and commented on enough for two lifetimes. He didn't need anyone else's opinion on what he should be doing. Since his divorce he'd had plenty of well-meaning friends try to set him up. He'd dated but nothing had stuck. He wasn't ready, hadn't been interested. But suddenly he found he was interested. Very interested.

Ali was in her office, having just given Emma her second steroid injection for the babies' lungs, when her phone buzzed.

She read the message.

Coffee? Perc Up—four p.m.?

The message had gone to a group chat, which included Ali and three girlfriends— Ivy, Harper and Phoebe—who had all met at medical school. They had now been friends for over twenty years, but it was only recently that they'd all been in the same city again. And not only were they all in Sydney, they were all working at Sydney Central Hospital as heads of their respective departments. Some days, Ali still found that difficult to comprehend. Not because she doubted her ability—it had been her goal to achieve this career highpoint and she'd worked hard for it—but to be able to realise it, as an Indigenous woman, was something special. Something she was very proud of. And to have four women heading up departments in the same hospital was a thrill, especially given their friendship. It made working together easy and fun. Ivy was Head of General Surgery and Harper the new head of the emergency department but Ali worked most closely with Phoebe, who was Head of Neonatal Surgery.

She needed a coffee and she wanted to

catch up on Ivy's news. She 'liked' the message and sorted herself, knowing she had time for a break as she'd be working late anyway. As usual.

Ali deliberately delayed her arrival at the café by a few minutes. Since Harper had returned from the UK their friendship remained a little strained and Ali was still reluctant to be in a situation where she and Harper were alone together. They'd been as close as sisters once upon a time, before Harper had started dating Ali's twin brother, Yarran. Before Harper had broken Yarran's heart when she'd rejected his marriage proposal in favour of a job in London.

She'd left without a word, to either Yarran or Ali, leaving them both in pain, breaking her friendship with Ali at the same time as breaking Yarran's heart. But where Ali felt betrayed, Yarran had been devastated and his heartache hadn't ended there. While he'd eventually got over Harper, married Marnie and had a little boy, he'd then found himself widowed, dealing with his wife's death and becoming a single parent. Ali blamed Harper for that too.

She knew she was being unreasonable but, in her mind, if Harper had accepted Yarran's proposal, if she'd stayed in Sydney, Yarran wouldn't have gone through any of that pain. She knew Yarran would say the pain was worth it though because without those events he wouldn't have his son, Jarrah.

But now Harper had returned from London and she and Yarran had found their way back to each other. They were engaged to be married. Ali wanted to support Yarran's decisions, but she was still trying to sort through her own feelings. She knew Yarran and Harper's relationship was really nothing to do with her, Yarran's happiness should be all that mattered, but she worried. She didn't want to see him hurt again. He was the most important person in Ali's life. Older than him by five minutes, she had always been very protective of him, but he obviously trusted Harper and Ali would have to trust Yarran's judgement. Trust that Harper wouldn't break her twin's heart a second time.

She also hadn't quite forgiven Harper for not saying goodbye to her. She knew she would have to put the past behind her because Harper was, all these years later, going to be part of her family and, for Yarran's sake and the sake of family unity, Ali knew she'd have to find a way of dealing with her own feelings of betrayal.

Ali had to adjust and accept. She'd have to forgive, if not forget. It would be difficult but she'd do her best. For Yarran's sake.

But for now, Ali had decided the best course of action was to avoid being alone with Harper. Until she'd achieved forgiveness and reached acceptance, she was best off avoiding any situation where she might put her foot in her mouth. The last thing she wanted to do was upset Yarran.

Ali was relieved to see that all three women had arrived before her, and Ivy, Harper and Phoebe were sitting on the leather Chesterfield couches by one of the large windows overlooking the street. Perc Up had comfortable seating, natural light, and myriad indoor plants gave the café a relaxing, peaceful vibe, far removed from the harsh artificial lights and noisy, bustling atmosphere of the hospital.

'Hi, have you ordered?' Ali asked as she dropped her handbag onto a couch.

'Harper and I have. Phoebe just sat down,' Ivy replied.

'I'll order for you, Phoebs, your usual?'

Phoebe shook her head. 'Can I have a peppermint tea?'

Ali frowned. 'No coffee?'

'I'm trying to cut down on my caffeine intake. It's getting a bit out of control.'

'You don't want decaf?'

Phoebe pulled a face and Ali laughed. 'Point taken. Peppermint tea coming up.'

'How is Emma today?' Ivy asked when Ali returned from the counter.

'Her blood pressure is still high but she hasn't developed any other concerning symptoms. Not yet anyway.' Ali knocked her knuckles twice on the wooden coffee table.

'Are you talking about Emma Wilson?' Harper asked. 'What's happened?' she added when Ivy nodded.

'She's developed pre-eclampsia,' Ali replied. Most of the hospital staff were aware of Emma's accident. Her story had been reported on in great detail by the media but as Head of the Emergency Department, Harper hadn't treated Emma since she'd first been brought into Sydney Central. 'And I'm hoping to buy her some more time before delivering her babies.'

'How many weeks is she?' Phoebe asked. Ali hoped Emma wouldn't need to consult Phoebe but, seeing as Phoebe was Head of Neonatal Surgery, it wasn't out of the realm of possibility that Emma, and her twins, would cross paths with her too. Especially if the twins were born several weeks early.

'Just at the end of thirty-two weeks. I've given her a second dose of corticosteroids today and now it's just a matter of time. I'm planning to wait as long as possible but, as you all know, there's not much I can do.'

'Did you get hold of Jake Ryan?' Ivy asked.

'I did. He came to my office last night.' She could feel the heat rising in her face as she recalled his chiselled features, easy smile and relaxed manner. Ali was pleased she had a dark complexion that hid her response to the memory.

'What did you think?'

'He seems competent.' Ali tried for a neutral response. Something professional.

'That's one word to describe him,' Ivy said with a smile. 'Tall, dark and handsome would be three others.'

'I hadn't noticed,' Ali replied with a grin.

'Liar.' Ivy laughed.

'Okay, I'll admit he was pretty easy on the eye.' She knew there was no point pretending he wasn't gorgeous. She might be forty years old but that didn't mean she wouldn't notice a good-looking guy and there had never been any topics that were off limits between the four of them. At least not until Harper had broken that trust…but that wasn't Ivy's fault.

'I don't know Jake,' Phoebe said, 'but he might be horrified to hear you girls talking about him like that.'

'He's relatively new,' Ivy replied as the waiter delivered their order. 'I think he's been at the Central for about three months, but don't worry, Phoebs, we're not objectifying him. He's also intelligent and charming and he's got a fabulous bedside manner.'

'He's an anaesthetist,' Harper cut in. 'His patients are asleep. He hardly needs much of a bedside manner for that!'

Ivy laughed. 'Fair call, but my point is he seems to be the whole package, but if you're not interested, Ali, I can introduce him to Phoebe. He's too good to let go.'

'Is he even single?' Ali shouldn't be asking but she had to admit she was curious to know the answer. She'd been curious since last night. 'Given how eligible he sounds, that would be surprising.'

'I haven't asked him directly,' Ivy answered, 'but nursing staff usually have their fingers on the pulse when any hot new colleagues appear and they seem to think he's eligible. I can find out for you. It's time you started dating again, don't you think? I'm not saying it has to be Jake,' she added when Ali stayed silent, 'but you would look good together. He's pretty cute.'

'Have you forgotten you're engaged to Lucas?' Ali said, trying to divert the focus of the conversation away from her love life, or lack of, and Jake. For some reason it was making her uncomfortable.

'Not at all. But just because I'm getting married doesn't mean I've lost all my senses. My eyes still work. But speaking of Lucas, that's why I wanted to catch up with you all. I wanted to know if you're free on Saturday night,' she said as she looked around the circle. 'Lucas and I were thinking of having drinks to celebrate our engagement. I know it's short notice but I don't want to have drinks without the three of you there. I feel like we haven't seen each other properly for ages.'

'That is short notice,' Harper said. 'What's the hurry?'

'Lucas thinks it would be nice to do something to mark the occasion but it seemed silly to have a big engagement party seeing as we want to get married in a few weeks, so we decided on casual drinks.'

'This Saturday?' Phoebe asked.

Ivy nodded. 'Yes. Are you free? I really want you all to be there.'

Ivy was the most sociable one of the four friends. The one who had always organised the parties. Ali suspected that Ivy used her busyness as a shield. As long as she was in the thick of things, camouflaged by her surroundings, people didn't look too closely at her.

'I'm free,' Harper said, 'and I think Yarran is rostered off but I'll check.'

Phoebe had her phone in her hand. 'My diary is clear,' she said as she looked up from the screen.

Ali didn't need to check her schedule to know the answer. 'I'm free too,' she said, not without a little disappointment. 'My social life is non-existent unless you count our family birthday parties and Sunday barbecues.'

'Maybe you'll meet someone at the party,' Ivy said. 'Lucas has some single friends. I'll make sure they're invited.'

'I hope Lucas's friends are a higher calibre of human than Adam is,' Ali said. Her ex had cheated on her and then left her. She'd thought they'd wanted the same things in life, thought they had the same goals and aspirations, only to find out that he wanted those things but not with her. Her confidence had taken a hiding and her subsequent trust issues meant she'd struggled on the dating scene since her divorce. Harper's betrayal hadn't helped either.

But she was lonely and, if pushed, she'd admit she'd like some company. Yarran had Harper... Ivy had Lucas. Phoebe was the only other member of their little group who was also single. It would be nice to be part of a couple again but she wasn't sure she had the energy for a relationship. Not unless it was easy. And it *should* be easy, shouldn't it? But she knew she wouldn't say no to good sex. And she could have that without a relationship. Maybe the party would be perfect timing.

'I'm sure he can rustle up some decent men,' Ivy was saying. 'One for you, Ali, and one for you, Phoebs.'

'Don't worry about me, I'm not looking for anyone,' Phoebe replied.

'Ooh, did you meet someone at the conference?' Ivy asked.

Phoebe shook her head as she picked up her cup and sipped her tea, successfully avoiding answering Ivy's question. Ali wasn't sure if anyone else noticed, and it could have been coincidental, but she was sure Phoebe had dodged the question on purpose. But it was the sort of tactic Ali had employed herself in the past so, while she filed the thought away and vowed to get to the bottom of it later, she took pity on Phoebe in the short term and changed the subject. 'How was the conference, Phoebs? I don't think I've asked you.'

'It was actually really good. There were some interesting speakers and a few surgeons were trialling some innovative techniques.'

'I see you're following Zac Archer on his social media,' Harper said. 'Did you meet him? He's supposed to be a brilliant surgeon.'

Phoebe nodded. 'I got to watch him perform heart surgery on a newborn. He was incredible.' Phoebe's eyes were shining and, as interesting as surgery could be, Ali found it hard to believe she'd be quite so excited by a surgical procedure.

'So, just some options for Ali, then,' Ivy said, refusing to be deterred from her self-appointed role as matchmaker.

'Please don't make it obvious that I'm a single woman,' Ali said. 'I'm happy on my own.'

'That's what I said and look at me now,' Ivy said as she stretched out her left arm to admire her engagement ring.

'I'm happy for you and Lucas. But, I promise, I'm fine.'

'You said your social calendar is looking bleak.'

'It is. But work's really busy and I don't have the time or the energy to date.'

'Ali, you're forty, not a hundred,' Ivy persisted.

'I've just found the last dates I've gone on to be hard work. And they shouldn't be. It should be easy. Exciting. Not exasperating or excruciating.'

'Think of dating as a challenge. You've never backed down from a challenge before.'

'I'd rather challenge myself in other ways.'

'And when was the last time you did that?'

She wasn't sure. 'When I accepted the job as Head of Obstetrics and Gynaecology,' she said, unable to think of anything more recent.

'So, months ago. I'll make a deal with you,' Ivy countered. 'I won't set you up with anyone but next time an opportunity presents itself for you to step out of your comfort zone or try something new—be it an invitation to dinner or an activity—you say yes. I don't like to think of you sitting at home alone.'

'Ivy, I'm fine.'

'I know. But there's no harm in having some fun.'

CHAPTER THREE

ALI WALKED INTO the hospital just as the sun was barely over the horizon. She was always there early, wanting to be on hand when the doctors did their rounds, wanting to be present, in case there were issues, but this morning she was earlier than usual. Unable to sleep, she'd woken before sunrise, her mind going over Emma's situation. Feeling uneasy and unable to go back to sleep, she'd gone for a run, showered and when she was still feeling twitchy she decided to listen to her sixth sense and go to work.

She had moved Emma up to the labour ward on the fourth floor and when she exited the lift she bypassed her office and headed towards Emma's room.

'Dr Edwards!' One of the nurses called out to her as she approached the nurses' station. 'Has someone already phoned you?'

Ali could feel goosebumps rising on her

forearms, making the fine hair on her arms stand up. 'No. What is it?' she asked, even though she could guess the problem.

'Emma Wilson is complaining of a headache. Pain relief isn't helping and she's just reported that her vision is blurry.'

'What was her blood pressure at the last reading?'

'One-ninety over one hundred and twenty.'

Ali turned on her heel. 'Come with me,' she called back over her shoulder to the nurse, not waiting to make sure her instructions were followed as she hurried to Emma's room.

She slowed down as she approached Emma's door. She didn't want to barge in like a whirlwind and frighten her patient. She needed to keep her as calm as possible.

'Good morning, Emma.'

Emma was lying in bed, eyes closed, her hands clenched into two fists, but she opened her eyes when she heard Ali's voice. Ali could see the pain in her eyes and noticed it took Emma a moment to focus on where she stood. Aware she would appear blurry, she moved closer to the bed.

'Dr Edwards.' Emma's jaw was tight, it was obvious that speaking was painful too, perhaps moving her jaw aggravated her headache.

'I hear you're not feeling so great,' Ali said as she looked at Emma's hands. They were swollen now, her fingers puffy, the skin stretched tight.

Her condition had deteriorated overnight and Ali wondered why no one had alerted her. But regardless of that, she should have come in when she first woke up. She'd known something wasn't right. She just hoped she hadn't left things too late.

There were a couple of things in her favour. Emma was conscious. She hadn't had a seizure. They were small things to be grateful for, but Ali would take anything at this point.

'I'm just going to take your blood pressure,' she said. The cuff was already wrapped around Emma's arm and Ali hit the button on the machine to inflate it. 'You've got a headache and blurred vision?'

Emma started to nod her head before stopping and choosing to answer verbally instead. 'Yes.' Maybe talking was the lesser of two evils.

'Any other new symptoms? Nausea, difficulty breathing?'

'No.' Emma's voice was just above a whisper.

'I'm just going to listen to your breathing,' Ali said as she placed her stethoscope on Emma's chest while she kept an eye on the blood-pressure reading. She'd already made the decision to take Emma to Theatre when the machine beeped. She checked the reading—one-ninety-five over one hundred and twenty.

'Emma, your condition is deteriorating. I need to deliver the babies.' Ali spoke slowly and softly. She didn't want to alarm Emma— her condition was precarious enough without adding fear into the mix.

'Today? We can't wait?'

Ali shook her head. 'I'm afraid not. Time is critical. Your blood pressure is climbing and headaches and blurred vision can precede a seizure. That's dangerous and it could be fatal. I promised you I'd do what's best for you and your babies. This is best. Waiting could put your life at risk and would likely mean an emergency caesarean. That would mean a general anaesthetic, another one, which I'd rather avoid, but more importantly if we do it now you can have a spinal block, which means you'll be awake when I deliver the babies and you should be able to hold them, all going well. It will be a far more positive experience for you and Aaron, less traumatic, better memories. If we do it now Aaron can be with you. In an emergency situation that would be very unlikely. I'm not going to risk your life or your babies. There will be a team of specialists in Theatre with me. This is the safest option. For all of you.'

'Okay.' Emma was clearly not capable of concentrating or focusing but she acquiesced quickly, another indication she was too sick to argue.

'I'll call Aaron and get him in here as quickly as possible while we get you prepped for Theatre.'

Jake had been called and he was already scrubbing at the sink outside Theatre when Ali walked in. She stood beside him, flicking the tap on and running the water over her hands and forearms.

He turned his head and smiled at her and as their eyes met Ali had a strange sensation of being hot and cold at the same time. She could feel tiny goosebumps on her skin yet she could also feel warmth spreading through her limbs and belly, as if she could feel her blood flowing through her veins.

'We meet again,' he said. 'I was looking forward to seeing you again but also hoping for it not to be here.'

Ali's stomach flip-flopped as he smiled at her. She was surprised again by how attractive she found him. She'd thought she'd committed his face to memory but it turned out she was wrong. He was gorgeous and when he smiled he just looked even more handsome.

'Not ideal, I agree,' she replied before she turned away, not wanting him to see her flustered. She squirted her hands with soap and started rubbing vigorously as Jake continued talking.

'I've spoken to Emma,' he said. 'She's got a canula in and I've given her something to relax her. I'm hoping that might also help with her headache and the spinal block should drop her BP too.'

Through the window above the sink Ali could see Emma was already in Theatre, her hand clasped tightly in Aaron's. Ali had explained the urgency of the situation to Aaron, explained that he could lose Emma if they waited. He'd been concerned about the babies but she'd reassured him they had an excellent chance of survival. A ninety-five per cent chance according to the statistics.

She didn't want to think about the other five per cent.

Lost in her thoughts, she didn't notice that Jake had finished scrubbing and she was in his way as he turned from the sink to dry his hands. His hip bumped against hers and the brief contact triggered a sense of unsteadiness. She felt unbalanced, unsettled, even though she knew she was stable. She needed to focus. She had a surgery to perform.

She had to concentrate. She took a deep breath as she gathered her thoughts.

'You okay?' Jake asked.

Ali nodded. 'I wish I didn't need to do this but it's the only option.' Using work as an excuse was the safest way to answer. She wasn't about to tell him that she'd be fine if he weren't around upsetting her equilibrium and disturbing her train of thought. Maybe it was a mistake to have asked him to be the anaesthetist.

'We've got this,' he said.

He uttered three simple words that made Ali feel as if she was part of a team. The team she'd told Emma about. Ali would be the surgeon but she wasn't doing this alone. The team were experienced. She had support. She'd asked Jake for help because Ivy had suggested it. Because Jake was good at his job. That was what Ali needed. What Emma needed.

Jake was a colleague, one of several who would be in Theatre with her. She could handle this. She could put aside her feelings, she was good at that, she could push them aside to deal with later. Much later.

'Ready?'

She looked up and met his gaze and nodded. 'Ready.'

They walked into Theatre together. The last to arrive. The operating room was full—Ali, Jake, Paul Minter, the paediatrician, an obstetrics registrar, Aaron, a nurse and two midwives, one for each baby.

'How are you feeling, Emma?'

'A little sleepy. I will be awake for the delivery, won't I? I don't want to miss this.'

Ali nodded. 'If everything goes to plan, yes, you will.' She wasn't about to make a promise she might not be able to keep but she was determined to give Emma the best experience she could in the circumstances.

'She'll be okay after this?' Aaron asked.

'Emma's blood pressure and all other symptoms should resolve quickly once we deliver your babies,' Ali reassured them.

'Can you turn onto your left side, Emma, and curl your knees up? I'm going to start the spinal block,' Jake said. 'You'll feel a little prick, some pressure, then a cold sensation. The block will numb you from the waist down but it will take a few minutes to have effect.'

'Once you're numb I'll make two horizontal incisions, both about ten centimetres long.' Ali stood in front of Emma and held up her fingers indicating the distance, talking to her patient, keeping her distracted, as Jake worked behind her. 'One in your abdomen and one in your uterus. We'll set up a screen so that you and Aaron won't see any of that. I'm sure you've seen babies delivered by C-section on television but, in my opinion, parents don't need to see that in real life. We're only creating beautiful memories today.'

Emma was rolled back into a supine position as the nurse and the registrar erected the screen just below Emma's chest, blocking her line of sight.

'Okay, Aaron, your position is up here with me, on this side of the drape where you can continue to hold Emma's hand,' Jake instructed. 'And if you've got Emma's playlist on your phone, I'll get that connected through the speakers for you.'

Aaron would be able to take photos and

play the music Emma had chosen in her birthing plan—another bonus of not having to undergo an emergency procedure.

'I love this song,' Jake said as the music started to play. He sang along to the first few lines as everyone laughed, easing the slight tension that always seemed to be present in the moments before a surgery commenced. 'What? Can't you see me in a boy band.'

Actually, it wasn't hard to imagine, Ali thought. He had a good voice. She could picture him twenty years ago, up on a stage, with all the girls, and some men too no doubt, in the front row hanging off his every word and movement. He commanded attention and he'd certainly caught her with his engaging smile and easy, relaxed manner.

'The performing arts' loss is medicine's gain,' she quipped, keeping the conversation light.

'Just be glad Emma didn't pick opera. That's not my forte.'

Ali picked up a pair of forceps and some gauze and looked at Jake, wanting to know if the anaesthetic would have taken effect. He nodded and Ali dipped the gauze in cold antiseptic solution before wiping it over Emma's skin. She didn't react but Ali double-checked, just in case.

'You can't feel that, Emma?'

'No.'

Ali swapped the forceps for a scalpel. 'You might feel a little bit of pressure with the cuts but no pain. Any discomfort, let me know.'

Ali concentrated, blocking out the sound of the music, as she prepared to start. Fortunately, Jake had stopped singing. His voice was good but she knew it would distract her.

She made a small initial cut, giving Emma a chance to object if she felt any discomfort.

'Do you know if the babies are girls or boys?' Jake was chatting to Emma and Aaron as Ali worked.

'Girls.'

'Have you picked out names?'

'Twin One is Jasmine and Twin Two is Poppy.'

'Have you got that, Dr Edwards? Don't mix them up!' Jake teased.

Ali looked up and met Jake's gaze. She could see the crinkles at the corners of his eyes above his mask and knew he was smiling.

'Got it.' Ali smiled back.

The registrar and the theatre nurse kept the incision clear, mopping up blood and cauterising vessels.

'And that's perfect timing and a perfect

baby,' she said as she lifted the first twin out. She held her behind the sheet as the registrar clamped the cord before holding her up for Emma and Aaron to see. 'Mum and Dad, meet Jasmine.'

Jasmine cried on cue. It wasn't a lusty, full-bellied cry but not bad for a premmie baby.

Emma had tears in her eyes but she didn't bother wiping them away. She held her hands out towards Ali, reaching for her daughter.

'We'll quicky get her checked over and cleaned up,' Ali said. 'Then you should be able to hold her.'

'Aaron, did you want to cut the cord?' Ali asked once the cord had stopped pulsating.

'I think I'll stay up this end, thanks.'

The registrar cut the cord and then Ali handed Jasmine to the midwife. 'Now for the next one.'

Ali repeated the procedure to deliver baby Poppy. She lifted Poppy up as the midwife brought Jasmine back and laid her on Emma's chest.

Poppy was noticeably smaller than her sister and her cries were softer, a little mewl like a newborn kitten, but both girls looked perfect. Ali handed Poppy to the second midwife and took a minute to watch Emma and

Aaron as they looked in total amazement at their daughter lying on Emma's chest.

'She's so tiny,' Aaron said.

'And so fair. I wasn't expecting that,' Emma said.

'That's not unusual,' Ali told her. Like Ali, Aaron was Indigenous, but it was common for babies with mixed parentage, Caucasian and Aboriginal, to be quite fair skinned at birth. 'She's got her dad's dark eyes and her complexion may change as she gets older. I've seen it in my own nieces and nephews.'

'She's perfect. They both are,' Aaron said as the midwife brought Poppy over and handed her to Aaron. 'Well done us,' he said as he bent down to kiss his wife.

Ali had to agree with him. Jasmine and Poppy were gorgeous babies. Small with perfectly shaped round heads, ten fingers and ten toes, pale eyelashes and dark eyes. After all the tragedy and horror, it was such a beautiful moment to witness—the start of Emma and Aaron's journey as parents, as a family. Ali did love babies—other people's—and she always felt privileged to be part of these moments in people's lives.

She lifted her eyes from the family tableau and once again her gaze met Jake's. As if they were perfectly in sync.

Was he thinking the same as her? About how amazing this was? Or did he know what it was like? She had no idea and, despite what Ivy thought, he could easily be in a relationship. He could have a family. A partner.

She found she really, really wanted him to be single.

He was still watching her and she realised she had been holding his gaze a little too long. She really had to stop doing that! Once again, she had the feeling he could read her thoughts. And she did not want him to know what she was thinking about right now.

She quickly looked away, intent on finding something else to occupy herself with. She busied herself delivering the placentas and checked the dosage of pain relief before it was injected through Emma's drip as one of the midwives took some family snaps with Aaron's phone before she took Jasmine away to do her five-minute Apgar score and measurements.

Emma was completely oblivious to what was happening to her now, she was totally focused on watching the midwife and paediatrician as they checked the babies. Listening as they relayed the measurements.

Ali listened too as she checked the board, making sure all the instruments and supplies were accounted for before she sutured the incisions.

At twenty-eight centimetres and seventeen hundred grams, Jasmine was slightly longer and heavier than Poppy. Poppy's second Apgar scores were also a little lower than Jasmine's. Her colour wasn't quite as good and her cries weren't as strong but her score was reasonable. In addition, her respiration rate was faster than Jasmine's but her oxygen levels were lower. Ali doubted Emma and Aaron would pick up on the difference but she heard the numbers.

'We're going to take the babies to the neonatal intensive care unit,' the paediatrician told Emma.

'Intensive care?'

'It's routine with what we call moderate preterm infants born between thirty-two and thirty-four weeks,' Paul reassured her. 'Poppy's oxygen is a bit low so we're going to supplement that for her.'

'Is she okay?'

'She's fine. We'll keep an eye on her. Once you're cleaned up, we'll get you into a wheelchair and bring you to the NICU.'

Ali tied off the sutures and stuck a dressing over Emma's wound. The edges had come together nicely and Emma's scar should be quite discreet once the incision healed. She let the registrar attend to Emma's post-surgical care.

'Your vitals are looking better, Emma, and your wound has come together nicely. It could take ninety minutes or so before you get the feeling back below your waist so we'll put a catheter in for you and then get you into a wheelchair so you can visit your daughters.'

Ali waited until Emma was safely transferred into the chair and was heading for the NICU with Aaron before going to change.

'That went well,' Jake said as they stripped off their protective layers.

'It went okay,' Ali said as she threw her gown into the linen skip.

'Surely you can relax now. You delivered two healthy babies.'

She could feel a little frown between her eyebrows and a little niggle of disquiet in her mind.

'What is it?' Jake asked.

'I'm concerned about Poppy's oxygen levels. They're not unusual for a small premmie baby but they're not as good as Jasmine's.'

'Should they be the same?'

'Not necessarily. But I'd prefer it if they were both good. I'm just worried about her lungs. Wondering if the steroids had time to help.'

'You did your best. It's impossible to control everything and it's unrealistic to think you can.'

'I know. Believe me, I know.' Sometimes she felt as if she wasn't in control of anything. But work was her happy place. Where she knew what she was doing. Where she felt as if she was on top of things. As opposed to her personal life. 'Emma has been through so much. I wanted to help her.'

'You did help her.'

'I would have preferred *not* to deliver her babies, though. Not yet anyway.'

'I think we both know it's not a perfect world. Don't beat yourself up about it. Emma is fine. You delivered two healthy babies. Everyone survived. Sometimes that's even better than we can hope for.'

She knew how lucky Emma was to have survived. The twins too. She just hoped they'd keep surviving.

'If you need to download, call me. You have my number,' he said.

Ali nodded. 'Thank you.' Her heart was racing but at least her voice sounded normal.

* * *

'You're doing well, Emma,' Ali said as she completed her day one post-surgical check.

She was moving slowly but her wound looked good, she was afebrile and her blood pressure was back to normal.

'How are Jasmine and Poppy? Have you been able to hold them?' Ali asked. She'd walked past the NICU on the way to Emma's room but hadn't gone in. Emma was her patient but the babies were under the care of the paediatrician. They weren't her responsibility even though she didn't always feel that way.

Tears welled in Emma's eyes, catching Ali off guard. Ali expected her to feel a little fragile after all the trauma she'd been through recently but the post-baby blues shouldn't have hit her this quickly. Something else must be happening.

Ali looked at Aaron, hoping for a clue as to what was going on, but he also looked close to tears.

'I've been able to hold Jasmine but Poppy has been having some trouble with her breathing so I've only been able to touch her while she's in her crib. She needs me, I know she does, and it's breaking my heart not to be able to hold them both.'

'What sort of trouble is she having?' Ali's throat felt tight, her mouth dry as her concerns about the babies' lungs rose to the fore again.

'Dr Minter said her breathing rate is still high compared to Jasmine. He thinks she might have something wrong with her heart. He was organising an ultrasound, I've forgotten what it's called, the one that shows the blood flow through the heart?'

'An echocardiogram,' Ali told her just as Paul Minter walked into the room. All eyes turned to him.

He was smiling and Ali relaxed. Whatever it was Paul's expression was telling them he could handle it.

'The results of Poppy's scans are back.' Ali, Emma and Aaron all waited silently for him to continue. 'As I suspect they show an issue with Poppy's heart, *but*,' he stressed, trying to keep everyone calm, 'it can be fixed.'

'What is it? What's wrong with her?' Aaron and Emma spoke in unison.

'She has a ventricular septal defect—big words, I know, but it's what's usually referred to as a hole in the heart.'

'A hole in her heart!' Emma cried.

'It's not uncommon and, as I said, it can be fixed.'

'But I had lots of ultrasounds while I was pregnant. I had one just three days ago. Why didn't this show up on any of those?'

'Depending on the size of the hole it's often not detected until after birth and, with twins, it's more difficult to diagnose in utero as the babies can get in each other's way and obstruct the sound waves. Sometimes these holes will close by themselves if they are small, but Poppy's hole is on the larger side. If her vital signs stay elevated it's an indication that her heart is needing to work harder than it should be. I suspect she will need surgery to repair it.'

'What type of surgery?

'Open-heart surgery.'

'Open-heart surgery!' Emma repeated before turning to Ali. 'You told me the babies would be okay!'

Ali knew she hadn't actually said that. She'd said their chances of survival were very good, she hadn't ever promised that they would be completely fine.

'Emma, Aaron, this is fixable.' Paul got the new parents to return their attention to him, allowing Ali to breathe again. 'We can operate here in the hospital. I'll consult with

Dr Mason—she is Head of Neonatal Surgery—and I expect we will get a neonatal cardiac specialist to consult as well.'

'When will this happen?'

'I'll speak to Dr Mason today but I'm hoping we can wait until Poppy is a little stronger. Until she puts on a little bit of weight. She's safe in the NICU at the moment.'

Jake pushed open the door to the hospital's rooftop garden. He often came up here to catch some of Sydney's glorious sunshine. After years of living in Melbourne he was relishing the fact that Sydney often had beautiful, sunny winter days and he preferred to take his breaks outside.

It was rare to find the rooftop empty but there was a cool wind today and so there was only one other person on the roof. He smiled at his good fortune when he realised it was Ali.

He'd been impressed by her professional skills but he couldn't deny he also found her attractive. Lithe, dark, mysterious. Intelligent, beautiful and interesting. She was an intriguing combination.

But he doubted she was single. Women like that didn't tend to be.

He wondered if he should ask Ivy about

her. But then he thought of all the reasons why it was best not to. She was out of his league. Head of the department. Since his divorce he was dating, but only casually and he didn't think she was the type of woman to do casual dating. She seemed too in control. He also tried to avoid dating colleagues. He'd seen the mess it had got some of his friends into when their relationships soured, and he was still relatively new at Sydney Central. He just wanted to settle into his job. Find a house. Focus on sorting his life out post-divorce. He had a lot on his plate.

Ali was standing by the edge of the roof-top, running her hand through a cluster of tall, soft grasses, lost in thought staring out across the city. She looked vulnerable, lonely, but he wasn't sure why he got that feeling. She could just be thinking about what to have for lunch.

But as he drew nearer, he could tell she was upset. He wondered if he should give her some space but what if he could help her?

'Ali? Is everything okay?'

She spun around, her eyes wide. She obviously hadn't heard him approaching. She shook her head and he heard her voice catch in her throat when she spoke. 'I've just found out that one of Emma's daughters, Poppy, has a ventricular septal defect, a hole in her heart. She's going to need surgery.'

He took his phone out of his pocket and looked at the screen.

Ali frowned and said, 'What are you doing?'

'I told you to call me if you needed to download. I'm just seeing if I missed a call from you.'

'I didn't call you.'

'I can see that. Why not?'

'Did you really mean that?'

'Of course. I'm happy to talk. Or to listen. You know this isn't your fault, don't you? Delivering the twins early possibly saved Emma's life and it didn't cause the hole in Poppy's heart. There's nothing you could have done to change this situation.'

'But should I have picked it up earlier?'

'What difference would that have made?'

'It might have given Emma and Aaron time to prepare. It was just such a shock for them.'

Jake didn't know how it worked but he did know that Ali hadn't been Emma's obstetrician initially. 'Was that your job? You weren't Emma's original obstetrician, were you? If no one else picked it up, why is this on you?'

'I feel I let her down.'

'How?' Ali was obviously upset and he wanted to help her. To cheer her up and re-assure her. 'You saved Emma's life. I used to think that was what being a doctor was all about. That's why I wanted to become one. To save lives. Then I realised that doctors do so much more than that. We heal. Create life. Sometimes take one.

'I know most medicos don't think anaes-thetists build rapport with our patients in the same way as other doctors do, and that's true for the most part—we breeze in, ask a few questions and then try to keep everyone alive. No relationship but a lot of responsi-bility. But I've been the anaesthetist for all of Emma's surgeries so I feel like I've got to know her. Or her situation at least. All you can do is your job to the best of your ability. There's a lot of things that can go wrong but things went right yesterday. You did every-thing right.

'You need to reset yourself,' he continued. 'What do you do when you need to relax? When you want to get away from it all?'

'I run. I read. I catch up with friends and family.' He smiled and she paused. He watched as her eyebrows drew together in a frown. Even when she was glaring at him, she was still stunning. 'What are you smiling at?' she asked.

'Just thinking we have very different ways of resetting,' he said.

'What do you do?'

'I climb things.'

She gave him a half-smile, which was better than a frown. 'What sort of things?'

'Big things.' He was grinning now. 'Rocks, cliffs, waterfalls. Those types of things.'

'That sounds dangerous...' Ali paused '...and not at all relaxing.'

'I didn't say I used it to relax. Just to reset and refocus. You can't think of anything else when you're fifty metres up a cliff face, clinging to a crevice by your fingers and toes. You have to focus. You have to problem-solve. You can't afford to be distracted. Every decision you make, from the route you choose, to where to place your hand, is magnified a hundred times. The smallest mistake, the tiniest hesitation, the littlest lapse of concentration can be disastrous.'

'I guess I can see how clinging to a vertical surface, several metres off the ground, could make you focus.'

'You should try it.'

Ali laughed. Jake was pleased to hear it. 'I think you need to work on your sales pitch if you expect anyone to try it after your description.'

'No, seriously, you should give it a go.'

'Why? Are you trying to kill me?'

'Not at all, but I figured you're the type of person who'd be up for a challenge.'

'Why would you think that?'

'You don't get to be the head of a department, especially at a young age, if you back away from a challenge.'

Ali wondered how old he thought she was, but she wasn't about to ask. He might think fifty was young.

'Here, have a look,' he said as he put his coffee cup down and pulled his phone out of his pocket. He scrolled through his pictures and held the device out to her. He swiped through a few pictures of him in what looked like various life-threatening positions on random cliff faces.

'You're not going to convince me to give it a go with those photos. The whole thing looks terrifying.'

'You wouldn't start with that. There are indoor climbing centres. They're safe, out of the weather, with people to train you. Give me your hands,' he said as he spun back to face her and reached out towards her.

Ali was puzzled but did as he asked. She put her hands in his. They were warm and gentle. He wrapped his fingers around her palms and his touch grounded her. She felt a similar connection when she was barefoot on the land. Grounded, connected to country. Now she was connected to Jake. It was a surprising sensation. A sense that her body already knew him from an earlier time, in an earlier place.

He lifted his hands and extended her arms away from her sides.

'What are you doing?'

'Checking your reach,' he replied. 'It's good.'

'Good for what?'

'Climbing. You're a good build for it. You've got long limbs and a light frame.'

She pulled her hands from his. She felt foolish, standing there holding onto him. 'I've got terrible upper-body strength.'

'You don't pull yourself up with your arms, your legs do the work. You just need a strong grip. There's a good climbing gym not far from here that I use for training. You should try it out.'

'Are you offering to teach me?' As the words left her mouth Ali realised with some mortification that he hadn't meant that at all.

She could tell by his expression that hadn't been his intention and her comment had taken him by surprise. 'Sorry, you weren't inviting me to go with you, were you?'

'It's okay, I've been trying to persuade you to give it a go so the least I can do is show you the ropes. I'm going tonight after work. Let me put the address in your phone and if you don't have babies to deliver and can get away you could meet me there,' he said, his words implying, very clearly, that it was up to her whether she went or not. That he wasn't inviting her on a date.

She didn't have plans for tonight and it was unlikely she'd be busy with a patient, but as she unlocked her phone and handed it to him, she thought maybe she could pretend to be held up at work and thereby avoid any awkwardness. But then she thought of Ivy telling her to take some risks, of the girls saying she liked a challenge, of Yarran and Harper finding love again, of Ivy and Lucas's whirlwind romance, and decided maybe it was time she did do something to shake up her life. Perhaps she would try rock climbing. But she didn't necessarily have to go with Jake.

CHAPTER FOUR

HER PLAN HAD been to search the internet for a different gym and to make some other enquiries. But that didn't explain how she found herself at Jake's gym nine hours later.

She'd gone home and grabbed her gym bag and thrown some things into it—with no idea what constituted suitable clothes, she'd assumed running gear would do—even while she had no real intention of climbing. And once she saw the wall she was pretty sure she wouldn't be persuaded to change her mind. Liking a challenge was one thing but this looked as terrifying as she'd imagined. More so.

The climbing walls were high, easily over ten metres and vertical, and the ones that weren't vertical were overhangs. She didn't think she had a fear of heights, she'd been on the hospital roof just today, but now she wasn't so sure.

The walls in the reception area were covered with long lists of rules and she baulked when the guy at the desk handed her a waiver to sign. She was just thinking about walking out when she heard her name.

'Ali. You made it. Are you feeling brave?'

She thought that might possibly be the worst thing he could have chosen to say. She swallowed, trying to dislodge the lump in her throat. 'I'm having second thoughts, to be honest. I didn't realise the walls would be so high and are those handholds on the ceiling?'

Jake laughed. 'Relax. They're for bouldering. You won't need to tackle those.'

'That's the good news.' She smiled even as she wondered if she was crazy to be here. But the upside of scaling a wall was getting to spend time with Jake and she had to admit she was finding him to be easy company.

But the really good news was that Jake was dressed for climbing. He was wearing shorts and a loose T-shirt, nothing fancy, but enough to reveal that his long legs were lean and muscular and his arms were toned. He looked good. He might be too young for her, definitely not in the demographic she was after, and he might not even be single, but that didn't mean she couldn't admire the view.

'You're here now,' he said. 'You might as well have a go. There are change rooms behind you and I'll meet you in the gym.'

Nothing ventured, nothing gained. He was right. She was here now. She got changed and took a deep breath, steeling herself to enter the gym. She saw Jake halfway across the cavernous space talking to another man.

'Ali, this is my cousin, Will,' he said as she walked up to them. 'Will, this is Ali, one of my colleagues.'

Ali thought Will looked a bit like Jake but when she shook Will's hand she was intrigued to find that, despite the similarity in looks, she didn't get the same sense of knowing Will as she did Jake. There was no sense of connection.

Ali knew this wasn't a date, she knew Jake hadn't really even meant to invite her, but she was still disappointed to realise she wouldn't have him to herself. 'I'm interrupting,' she said.

'No, not at all,' Will replied.

'Let's get you sorted,' Jake said. 'You picked up some shoes at the desk?'

Ali held up her left hand. 'These things?

I don't think I've ever seen shoes quite like these.'

'They help you to grip the handholds.'

'Hang on. I'll be gripping handholds with my feet?'

'It's not as hard as it sounds. Trust me.' Jake winked at her and her belly did a slow roll.

Ali wasn't convinced she should trust him but she was here now and it wasn't in her nature to give up. She sat on the ground to pull the shoes on. 'Okay, what's next?' she said as she stood up.

'You'll need a harness.' Will passed one to Jake and he stepped close, obviously about to attach the harness for her. His proximity made her nervous and she was about to say she could do it when she realised she couldn't. She had no clue where to start.

Jake bent down and spread the harness on the ground. 'Step into it,' he said, before sliding it up her legs after she'd done as he asked. His hands grazed the outside of her bare thighs before he reached the hem of her running shorts. Goosebumps sprang up even though his fingers were warm and her skin felt as if it were on fire. Her knees wobbled and she prayed her legs would support her. She didn't know how she was going to manage to haul herself up a wall—it felt as though all of her strength had deserted her.

He had moved to one side of her now and was talking so she forced herself to concentrate. He'd said rock climbing was all about focus and concentration, so she needed to heed his advice and pay attention.

'Tuck your shorts under the harness,' he told her. 'You don't want it rubbing on your skin.'

Thank God he had left that for her to do, she thought as she pushed the hem of her shorts under the harness straps at the top of her legs. She didn't think she could handle his hands touching the tops of her thighs. Next time she'd wear leggings, not shorts. Although depending on how tonight went there might not be a next time.

She held her breath as he reached his arms around her to clip the harness closed before tightening the straps.

'Last things, carabiners and a chalk bag.' He knelt down and clipped a carabiner onto her harness. 'That's for the safety rope,' he said, before attaching a soft bag filled with chalk dust. 'This helps with your grip if your hands get a bit sweaty. You probably won't need it, but I'll strap it on just in case. Okay, that's it. You're good to go.'

'I feel like a Christmas turkey. Trussed up and about to meet my maker.'

'I've been doing this for years. I won't let anything happen to you,' he said.

And she believed him.

'You're going to show me what to do first, right?' she asked.

Jake nodded. 'I'll send Will up the wall to demonstrate. That way I can talk you through what he's doing. It's not hard, I promise.'

She raised one eyebrow but kept quiet as Will clipped himself onto a rope and handed the end to Jake, who threaded it through his own harness.

'My job is to belay him.'

'To what?'

'Belay. It means I'm managing the rope for the climber. If he falls, I have to apply tension to counteract the fall. It's a safety mechanism. On belay!' he called out.

'Climbing,' Will responded.

'Climb on,' Jake said. He looked briefly at Ali, so she knew he was addressing her, before turning his attention back to his cousin. 'There's a lot of terminology in climbing, a lot of it for safety reasons, but it's not that important in an indoor setting. Outdoor climbing is more difficult because of the conditions. There are more things to watch out for—wind, falling rocks—and it's harder to hear.'

Ali watched in amazement as Will scaled the wall. He didn't race up but moved slowly and smoothly, his movements considered, and she could tell he was thinking about where to place his hands and feet.

'It looks more graceful than I imagined.'

'It's like doing ballet on a wall,' Jake agreed.

It wasn't the first time she'd seen rock climbing, but it was the first time she'd seen it in real life. It was also the first time she could get a real perspective of the height of the wall and the distance between the handholds. 'It also looks much more difficult.'

'Will is taking an intermediate route.' Jake spoke to her without taking his eyes off his cousin.

'That looks hard to me.'

'Don't worry. The routes are colour-coded according to difficulty. You'll start on an easy route. For example, look at the yellow holds on the adjacent wall, see how close together they are, and evenly spaced, almost like a ladder? That's a "very easy" route. The blue handholds on that wall are graded "easy". See how he's keeping his arms straight? Straight arms conserve energy. He's pushing himself up the wall with his legs. Watch how he keeps one hip close to the wall—that works with your centre of gravity, keeps your weight over your feet and brings your shoulder close to the wall, makes it harder to fall off and easier to grip.'

'Can I start on "very easy"?' she asked.

'I thought you liked a challenge,' he said as Will reached the top of the wall and Jake was able to take a moment to look at Ali.

'We'll see,' she replied with a smile. She wanted to appear confident. She wanted to impress Jake. Wanted him to think she was assured and capable. All around her people of all shapes and sizes were scaling the walls. Children, teenagers, people older than her. She'd put aside her reservations, she decided. What was the worst that could happen?

'Ready to lower,' Will called down.

'Lowering.'

Jake let out a short length of rope as Will sat back in his harness and started to walk down the wall.

'Are you ready to give it a go?' Jake asked once Will was back on the ground and had unclipped the rope.

Ali took a deep breath and exhaled slowly before nodding.

'Come over to this wall,' Jake directed. He threaded a rope through her harness as she stood at the base of the wall. 'This type of climb is called top roping, where the rope is attached at the top of the wall and you work with your belayer. That's me.' He grinned. 'Try the blue route. I promise it's not that difficult. The first thing you need to do is take a look at the route, plan your first ten grabs. That way you're less likely to get yourself tied up in knots. We're trying to move smoothly, to conserve energy, so you can make it to the top. You don't want to look like you're playing a game of Twister.'

'Aren't you supposed to be telling me this is easy, not telling me I'm likely to get tied up in knots?'

'You'll be fine. Women generally make good climbers. They use their brains and they seem to be able to do two things at once—climb and think a couple of steps ahead to avoid precarious situations. Men rely more on their brawn. They know that if they get themselves into a tricky spot their strength will usually get them out. Women tend to prefer to avoid getting themselves into those situations in the first place.'

'That sounds sensible.'

'If anything goes wrong, if you get stuck

and can't reach a handhold, just let go of the wall.'

'What? You want me to let go of the wall? Are you crazy?'

'I'll be controlling you. I can lower you down. There's nothing to worry about.'

'Hmph.' But she was smiling, she was almost excited now to give it a go.

'On belay!' Jake called out. 'Now you say "climbing", I say "climb on" and off you go.'

Ali stepped closer to the wall but looked over her shoulder at Jake before reaching up for the first handhold.

'Remember straight arms and keep your hip close.'

As she made her way up the first couple of feet she could hear Jake below her, suggesting which handhold to use as he controlled the rope. As she climbed higher, she was conscious of the view he had, looking straight up at her.

But she couldn't think about that. She had to concentrate. If she had to problem-solve, if she had to choose the handholds for herself, she didn't have time to worry about what Jake might be thinking as he looked up at her.

She blocked out Jake's voice and decided to make her own decisions.

She saw a handhold to her right and reached for it before figuring out it was both further than she thought and green. She should be looking for a blue handhold.

Her hip rotated away from the wall and she found herself swinging out into nothing as her right foot slipped. Her centre of gravity shifted and then her left foot slipped.

She was falling!

Her heart was in her mouth but before she could call out, she jerked to a stop.

Jake had stopped her fall. He'd said to trust him, he'd told her he'd keep her safe and he'd kept his word.

He lowered her to the ground. 'Are you okay?' he asked as her feet hit the matting on the floor.

'Yes.' She was breathing heavily and her heart was racing but she was okay. She'd only been a few feet off the ground and the floor was covered in thick foam matting— she doubted she would have done any damage, in any case, even if Jake hadn't been so quick to respond.

'Did you want to try again?' he asked.

'Definitely.' The adrenaline racing through her body made her ready for another challenge and she'd always been competitive. Growing up with a twin brother and a mother who had been a professional athlete, she'd always felt as though she had something to prove. Add being an Indigenous female into the mix and that only made her more determined to prove something to herself and to Jake. She was not going to give up at the first fall.

She glanced over to her left where several teenagers were scaling an adjacent wall. She wasn't going to let them show her up. She wanted to prove that a forty-year-old woman could do this.

She looked at Jake and waited for his instruction.

'On belay.'

'Climbing.'

She tried again, making sure to use only blue grips this time, and made it to the top of the wall.

'Well done,' Jake called up to her. 'Now you just have to get down.'

She looked back over her shoulder, at Jake. He looked a long way down. Right, she hadn't really thought this through.

'Sit back in the harness,' Jake told her, 'like you're sitting into a chair.'

She was nervous.

'I've got you,' he called up to her. 'You've got to trust me.' Trust was something she had difficulty with, but she realised she would have to do as he said if this wasn't going to go pear-shaped.

'Did I mention I have trust issues?'

'I've caught you once already,' Jake said. 'I'm not going to let anything happen to you. Sit back. Good! Now straighten your legs, keep your feet level with your hips. Remember how Will did it. Bend one knee a little and push off the wall with that foot, take a step down and repeat on the other side. I'll let the rope out, you just walk backwards down the wall.'

Jake talked her back down the wall. By the time her feet hit the ground she was smiling from ear to ear.

'I made it.' She was buzzing. She looked up at the wall. 'I can't believe I just climbed that.'

'You did great. I told you you'd be good at it.' He was grinning too, looking pleased with her effort, and Ali's heart skipped a beat. 'Did you think about work?'

'Are you kidding? Not at all,' she said as Jake began to unclip her harness. The harness dropped to the floor and she bent down to pick it up. 'Thank you, I enjoyed that. I wasn't sure that I would.' She'd surprised herself. She enjoyed the sense of achievement, but it was Jake's company that had made it a far better experience than it might otherwise have been.

'Let me take that,' Will offered, reaching for her harness. 'We're going to grab a quick bite to eat in Chinatown, why don't you join us?' he invited.

'I don't want to intrude,' she replied. She couldn't remember the last time she went out with new people. She spent time with her girlfriends and her family but avoided most other social interactions; her confidence had taken a hit when her marriage ended.

'You're not intruding. My partner Chris is meeting us and it would be nice to have extra company.'

Ali looked at Jake, wondering how he felt about his cousin's invitation. 'You're welcome to join us,' he said.

'Okay, thank you, that sounds good.' She wasn't ready for the night to end just yet. It was the most fun she'd had in a while.

Will and his partner, Chris, were good company. Jake was a little quiet and Ali worried that perhaps she shouldn't have joined them but maybe this was their usual dynamic.

Tall and well-groomed, Chris was certainly outgoing and chatty. He was also very well dressed, albeit with an edgy style, and Ali wasn't surprised to find he worked in theatre, specifically set design.

'Do you work in theatre as well, Will? Is that how you met?'

'We met through mutual friends. I'm an architect.'

'Commercial or residential?'

'Residential. The Sydney market keeps me busy.'

'And do you climb, Chris?' Ali asked, wondering why he hadn't joined them at the gym. She thought perhaps he'd been working.

'Honey, please.' Chris laughed. 'Have you seen the outfits? Those shoes! If I'm going to work up a sweat exercising, I am *not* going to do it in something so unfashionable.'

Ali would normally be offended if someone called her 'honey', but it was obviously just a figure of speech for Chris and delivered so dramatically she couldn't help but smile.

'Not to mention uncomfortable,' Chris continued. 'I prefer to get my exercise on the dance floor or in the bedroom.'

'Chris, that's a little too much information,' Will cautioned but Ali laughed.

'It's been ages since I went dancing.' And ages since her bedroom had seen any activity too, but that would definitely be too much information!

Dancing was an activity that cleared her mind—she hadn't thought of that when Jake had asked her the question. The last time she'd danced had been when she'd cleaned her apartment. She played music to pass the time but now that she lived in an apartment on her own it didn't take long to clean. It was minimalist and she didn't make much mess. She spent most of her time at work or at one of her siblings' houses. Her life wasn't at all exciting.

'You should take Ali dancing, Jake,' Will suggested.

'I don't dance,' he replied.

'I'll be your dance partner,' Chris offered.

'Thank you. I might take you up on that,' Ali said, 'once I recover from tonight's activities. My legs are starting to feel a little stiff.' She stretched her legs under the table, feeling the tightness in her calves. It had been fun, but Jake still seemed a little tense, maybe it was time to call it a night. 'Thanks for inviting me but I think I should head home and get in the shower if I'm going to be able to move tomorrow.'

She'd enjoyed the evening—it had been lovely not to talk about her work, her nieces and nephews, pregnancies, babies and her lack thereof.

'I'll walk you to your car,' Jake offered, leaving Ali slightly disappointed that he didn't try to talk her into staying longer.

'Thank you for tonight,' she said once they were alone. 'I needed that.' She knew Jake hadn't intended to invite her along, and she'd ended up spending the whole evening with him, but she was grateful as she'd enjoyed herself more than she had in a long time.

'Which part?'

'All of it. The climbing. The conversation. The company. A chance to get away from work. It was fun. I enjoyed it.'

'You're welcome any time. You can also go to the gym on your own if you want to. There will always be someone to belay you.'

'I'm not sure if I'll do it again but I appreciate you letting me join you tonight.' She knew there was no point getting caught up with Jake. And there was no point in going climbing again without him.

She had to admit she was attracted to him, and he was her type with one exception—he was too young. Her next partner would be older, past the age of wanting a family. She didn't want to get her heart trampled on again. She didn't want false promises, didn't want to be dumped for someone younger, someone of child-bearing age. The next time she dated someone *she* would be the younger woman.

'This is me.' She had her car keys in her hand and pushed the button on the fob to unlock the door.

Jake opened the driver's door for her and she stopped to thank him again before she got in. They were standing close together, him holding the door, and her pressed against the side of the car. If she wanted to, she could lean forward and kiss his cheek. His mouth.

She wondered what it would be like to kiss him. Maybe they could swap climbing for sex? That was an offer she knew she'd take up. She didn't need to date him for that. Maybe that was an option to consider.

CHAPTER FIVE

ALI HAD JUST left Emma's room after another follow-up check and had bumped into Ivy in the corridor on her way to see Emma. It seemed there were a lot of staff at the Central invested in Emma and her babies. As they chatted outside the NICU Ali saw Jake walking towards them. She could feel a blush staining her cheeks and hoped no one would notice.

'Jake,' Ivy said when she spotted him. 'What are you doing up here?'

'I'm looking for Aaron. Is he up here?'

Ali nodded as she willed her blush to fade. 'He's in with Emma,' she said.

'How is Emma going? And the twins?'

'They're okay,' Ali replied. 'Emma is able to hold Jasmine and also have a little bit of contact with Poppy. She's still on oxygen but stable.'

'I'm glad we bumped into you, Jake,' Ivy

said. 'I've been meaning to email you. Lucas and I are having a few people over tomorrow night for drinks to celebrate our engagement. We'd love you to join us if you're free? You're welcome to bring a date too, although there'll be plenty of people you know. Plenty of colleagues. Ali is coming.'

'Are you bringing a date?' He turned back to Ali. Strangely, she sensed that her answer to his question would determine whether he accepted Ivy's invitation or not.

She was nervous but she couldn't lie. 'No.'

A wide smile broke across Jake's handsome face and Ali felt as though a thousand butterflies had been released inside her belly.

'It sounds fun, thanks, Ivy. This is my first full weekend off since I started here. I'd love to come.'

'Good. All sorted. I'll email you the address.'

'OMG, I can't believe you just did that,' Ali said as Jake headed down the corridor to Emma's room.

'Did what?' Ivy said with an innocent tone, which was contradicted by a cheeky grin.

'You know exactly what. Inviting Jake to your drinks.' Ali knew Ivy had done it on her behalf and although she tried to be affronted, in reality all she felt was excitement tinged with a little nervousness. Had she and Jake just crossed a line? Committed to something unspoken? She felt ridiculous—forty years old and her hormones were running rampant.

Ivy laughed. 'You should be saying thank you. One of us might as well get to enjoy his company. I can tell you like him and you weren't going to invite him.'

'I can find my own dates.'

'I'm not saying you can't, but you said you weren't bringing one tomorrow night. I'm not making you turn up together and what happens next is completely up to you. I'm just putting the pieces in place. So, you're welcome.'

Ali and Phoebe arrived together at Lucas's apartment. Ivy's dress code had said 'Cocktail' and Ali was pleased she had a reason to make an effort. She wouldn't mind a bit of attention and it was nice to be able to swap her scrubs and gym gear for a pretty dress. Who knew who she might meet tonight? She pretended she hadn't chosen her outfit with Jake in mind, but that didn't stop her nerves from kicking in as the lift took her and Phoebe closer to the top floor. Would he already be there?

The lift had mirrored walls and she checked her reflection one final time before reaching her destination. Ivy had discussed in great detail how fancy Lucas's apartment was and Ali suspected the 'little drinks' could be an extravagant affair and had dressed accordingly. She wore a navy trench coat, to combat the winter evening chill, over a gold sequin shift dress that skimmed her slim figure and complemented her skin tone. She'd pulled her dark hair away from her face to show off her gold drop earrings. The only other jewellery she wore was a charm bracelet that had belonged to her gran.

The lift doors opened and Ali and Phoebe found themselves in Lucas's penthouse apartment. The apartment was stunning and Ali squeezed her jaw tight, afraid her mouth was going to gape open in wonder. She looked around, taking it all in—the large marble kitchen island under a statement pendant light, original artworks and the monochromatic colour scheme. Despite the colour scheme the apartment wasn't cold or austere, it felt inviting and comfortable. Soft couches, thick rugs and plenty of lamps were positioned around the room, giving the space an elegant ambiance.

The apartment was expansive and she couldn't help but think her entire apartment would fit into Lucas's kitchen and living area. She had been happy with the purchase of her own two-bedroom apartment, which she'd bought following her divorce. It was newly constructed, the right size for her—she didn't want to rattle around in something when she lived alone—and she'd enjoyed decorating it with new pieces of furniture mixed in with things she'd inherited that held special meaning. It had been a purchase she'd been proud of, one she'd handled on her own from finding the apartment to making the offer, arranging finance and moving in. After her divorce it had felt like a major achievement and she'd felt as if it had been a big step forward into her new life, but it could only be described as modest, especially compared to Lucas's.

Lucas's apartment was beautifully decorated, understated and tasteful and there was no hiding the fact that it must have been expensive. Not just the decor—the view alone was worth millions. Large sliding glass doors on the far side of the room had been opened to allow access to the generous balcony and, framed through the doorway, Ali could see the iconic Sydney view of the Harbour Bridge and the Opera House. It was incredible.

A DJ was set up towards one end of the room where the indoors merged with the outdoors and two bartenders had commandeered the kitchen island and were mixing cocktails and pouring champagne.

She didn't think she and Phoebe were late, although it had taken her longer than usual to get ready, but the apartment was already heaving with people. The majority of guests seemed to be hospital staff, which was not surprising, she thought, as Ivy came to welcome them.

Ali smiled; the party might have been Lucas's idea but Ivy had obviously run with it. She was the most sociable of the four girlfriends and she'd clearly invited everyone she could think of or had bumped into at the hospital. Including Jake.

The moment she thought of him was the moment the crowd shifted, as if sensing where her thoughts were headed. The guests parted, leaving her looking directly at Jake. He was talking to one of their colleagues but his eyes were on Ali.

A member of the wait staff offered to hang her coat up for her, distracting her momentarily, but she kept her eyes on Jake as she slipped it from her shoulders to reveal the gold sequin column dress she wore underneath. She saw Jake smile and hoped he appreciated her outfit, finally admitting to herself that she'd worn it with the hope it would catch his attention. She wanted to make a statement. Wearing scrubs or exercise gear might be practical but she wanted him to see what she could look like with a little bit of effort. She might be forty but she didn't want to be invisible.

He was still smiling as he started to cross the room. He came straight to her, not even pretending to stop and chat to anyone else as he made his way through the crowd. She was flattered. This was what she'd wanted although she hadn't been brave enough to admit it to herself until now.

She waited for him to reach her side, confident that her side was exactly where he was headed. His eyes hadn't left hers. She knew she was his destination.

Jake swiped two glasses of champagne from the tray of a roving wait staff as he passed by, handing one to her when he reached her side. Her pulse leapt as his fingers grazed hers and she was relieved that she didn't slosh champagne out of the glass as her hand trembled.

'Hello,' he greeted her. 'You look amazing.' There was no hesitation on his part, he obviously had no concerns about what to say and his comment gave her confidence.

She smiled, emboldened by the knowledge that she wasn't invisible. 'Thank you,' she replied as she decided she would be brave tonight. She would take a risk. Take an opportunity to get to know him better if the opportunity was presented to her and, looking at his expression, she suspected she might get that chance. His gaze was dark, intense and direct as he ran his eyes over her and Ali was grateful for the dim lighting as she felt her cheeks darken in response to his observation.

'Girls' night out?' he asked.

'Pardon?'

'I saw you and Phoebe arrive together. You didn't change your mind and bring a date?'

Belatedly she remembered she'd arrived with Phoebe, who was now nowhere to be seen. Both she and Ivy had completely disappeared. When had that happened?

'No date. No partner, no husband and no boyfriend,' she said, wanting to let him know she was single without actually saying the word. She wanted him to know she was available but didn't want to appear desperate. She *wasn't* desperate, she reminded herself. She was just a woman who hadn't had sex in a long time. Perhaps that was all about to change.

She sipped her champagne as she took Jake in. He was dressed all in black—his jeans, collared shirt and jacket were all black. His outfit made him look even taller and leaner than usual. She was wearing heels but he was still a couple of inches taller than her, but not too tall that she couldn't see into his eyes, not too tall that she couldn't watch his perfect lips move as he spoke to her.

He might appreciate her outfit but she also appreciated his. He looked sensational. The other male guests were all in suits and ties and she wondered if he was deliberately not conforming. 'You didn't get the dress code?' She smiled.

'A jacket is as close as I get to cocktail attire,' he said, making it clear he obviously did get the memo but had chosen to ignore it. 'I don't do ties.'

But rather than looking out of place he stood out for all the right reasons. His individual look ticked all of her boxes. 'It's been a while since I've seen anyone dressed all in black—it's a very Melbournian look,' she said. In contrast to the city of Melbourne,

Sydney weather, even in winter, was often too warm and sunny to embrace the dark colours of a traditional winter wardrobe. Sydneysiders would wear black but lighten the look with a shirt or scarf, tie or bag in a contrasting colour.

'I've just moved back here from Melbourne,' he said.

'You're from Sydney originally?' she asked as they slowly moved further into the apartment. They were surrounded by other guests now, but none of them were close acquaintances of Ali's and she felt as if she and Jake were existing in their own space.

'Yes. I'm still getting used to being back but it sounds like I need to update my wardrobe.'

'I'm not complaining,' she replied with a smile. He looked hot, there'd be no complaints from her. 'I was born here, I'm a proud Garigal woman,' she said, naming her mob. 'Black is my favourite colour.'

'Clever,' Jake replied with a smile that made Ali's insides melt. 'And I'm glad you approve.'

Oh, she definitely approved.

She was intrigued as to what had brought him back to Sydney but they were interrupted before she could ask the question.

'Hey, sis.'

Ali turned her head to find Yarran and Harper standing beside her. She saw Jake look from her to Yarran and then back as Yarran kissed her cheek.

Harper hugged Ali in greeting and Ali hugged her back, trying to ignore the slight awkwardness she still felt. She hoped that one day she wouldn't tense up remembering how things used to be between them. She hoped one day she wouldn't have these moments of hesitation around Harper.

'Hi, Jake,' Harper said as she released Ali and stepped back, reaching for Yarran's left hand. 'I don't think you've met Yarran. My fiancé and Ali's brother.'

'Your twin brother?' Jake asked Ali.

Ali nodded. Jake had asked about her siblings when they'd had dinner in Chinatown and she was pleased he'd remembered she was a twin.

'Yarran is a firefighter,' Harper continued. 'He's the one who rescued Emma Wilson.'

As Head of the ED Harper also saved lives for a living but Ali was pleased to hear the note of pride in Harper's voice as she introduced Yarran to Jake.

'It wasn't only me,' Yarran commented.

Harper looked at him adoringly, as if he

was the ultimate hero, and it made Ali feel better to see how much Harper clearly loved him. 'But you were the one who carried her out of the fire,' Harper said. 'Jake is an anaesthetist at the Central; he's looked after Emma too.'

'Jake Ryan,' Jake said as he shook Yarran's hand. 'It's good to meet you.'

'Jake Ryan? Why is your name familiar?'

'It's a fairly common name.'

'No. I've seen it somewhere recently.' Yarran frowned in concentration.

'Jake is organising the fundraiser at Circular Quay,' Harper said. 'The one your station is taking part in.'

'The abseiling challenge?'

Jake and Harper nodded in unison.

'What fundraiser?' Ali asked. She had no idea what they were talking about.

'It's a charity fundraiser for childhood cancer,' Jake replied.

Ali wondered why she didn't know about it if Yarran and Harper did. Had Harper deliberately not told her? Was she keeping Ali at arm's length, focusing on Yarran? Ali reminded herself that all she wanted for Yarran was happiness. Did it matter if her relationship with Harper didn't ever quite get back to what it was as long as Yarran was okay?

'Are you running it?' she asked Jake.

'No. But I'm on the committee and each year there are several fundraising events. I suggested this one so I'm one of the contact people, but the actual running of the event is outsourced. The company responsible has run something similar in Townsville, although it wasn't a fundraiser, it was an attempt to break a world record.'

'For what?'

'The largest number of abseilers in a twelve-hour period.'

'How many people was that?'

'Over thirteen hundred.'

'Wow! How did they find that many abseilers?'

'The majority of those participants had never abseiled before, so prior to the event they weren't abseilers, just participants. I'm hoping we can break the record again as it makes for good publicity. We're aiming for fourteen hundred people.'

'And how does the fundraising work?'

'People pay to enter and then we also ask them to get sponsors.'

'Are you doing it?' Ali asked Yarran.

'I am. There are a heap of emergency service personnel taking part,' Yarran replied. 'Don't worry, I'll be coming to you for sponsorship.'

'Oh, the DJ is paying our song,' Harper said as she took Yarran's hand. 'Come and dance with me.'

'Good to meet you, Jake,' Yarran said as he let Harper pull him away.

Ali turned her attention to Jake, curious to hear more about this charity event that everyone but her seemed aware of. 'How did you get involved with this charity?'

'Come and sit outside with me and I'll tell you. We should make the most of this view if it's not too cold.'

They stepped out onto Lucas's balcony. The night was clear, the air was cool but there was no breeze. They gravitated towards a small outdoor sofa and some chairs that were grouped around an ethanol firepit. The sofa faced the Harbour Bridge and had the added benefit of seating two people. Ali chose the sofa.

'Are you okay out here? Will you be warm enough?' Jake asked as he sat beside her.

She could feel the warmth of the fire and the heat coming off Jake's body, but it was still cool. Her dress was a sleeveless sheath, there wasn't much of it, and it offered little protection against the evening air. 'I probably should have grabbed my coat,' she said.

'Here. Take mine.'

She started to protest but Jake had already shrugged out of his jacket and was draping it around her shoulders. It was warm from his body heat and she stopped objecting as the fabric wrapped around her. 'Thank you, that's much better. Now, tell me more about this charity and what you do.'

'I got involved with the charity because I wanted to give back. Not just financially, I wanted to make a difference with my time and experience. And not only my experience or skills in medicine. This is personal for me. I had cancer as a child—I know what it's like.'

'You did?' A thousand questions swarmed through her mind—when, what, how serious was it and how was he now? 'How old were you?' she asked first.

'Four. I was diagnosed with a Wilm's tumour. Stage two.' Ali frowned. She knew Wilm's tumours were rare. 'The doctors removed one of my kidneys,' Jake continued, 'and I had chemo for twelve months.'

Ali put one hand on her chest and took a deep breath. 'That sounds traumatic.' She could only imagine how she would feel if one of her nieces or nephews had received a similar diagnosis.

'Kids are tough. Resilient. And it wasn't all bad,' he said with a smile. 'I survived. And my experience led me to a career in medicine. This is my way of giving something back. This was a way for me to be involved in something that resonates with me. A chance to make a difference. I feel I have something to contribute to the charity, but I really enjoy getting involved with the events that involve the children. I know what the kids are going through.'

'Are there kids doing the abseiling?'

'Over sixteens can sign up. This is an activity that is fun and doesn't take a lot of energy. Just a bit of courage and the kids have plenty of that. My experience with cancer is kind of how I got into climbing in the first place. My parents were advised to steer me away from contact sports as a child—things like rugby, soccer and football were deemed too risky with one kidney—so instead I swam, played tennis and was eventually introduced to climbing.'

'You're okay now?'

'For the time being. The survival rate is good but there may be related health issues later in life.' He shrugged. 'Life is short. I want to experience it all. I've been given a second chance. I intend to make the most of it.'

'So, your cancer experience introduced you to climbing *and* led you to medicine?'

He nodded.

'You weren't sick of hospitals?'

'No. Doctors and hospitals saved my life. I was good at science, so I thought I'd like to do the same—save lives.'

'So that's why you chose anaesthesiology?'

'I figured what better way to save someone's life than to be responsible for it? To literally hold someone's life in my hands, to anaesthetise them and be the one to make sure they come through the other side. I didn't realise until I was older that doctors do a lot more than save lives. They can help to create it, can mend lives and sometimes as an anaesthetist I've even had to take it away, but I like to think I make a difference. It's a big responsibility and I love it but there might have been a little bit of a selfish element to the speciality I chose.'

'What's that?'

'I don't have to sacrifice my whole life. It leaves time for other pursuits. It leaves time for me to live my life. It's important to me to make the most of my second chance at life. But now, I want to hear about you. You and Ivy are good friends?'

'Yes, Ivy and I met at uni. We studied with Harper and Phoebe.'

'All four of you? Together?' Ali nodded. 'Did you introduce Yarran and Harper?'

'Yes.'

'Has that caused some issues between you and Harper?'

'Why do you say that?'

'You seemed a little tense with her. Different from how you are around Ivy and from how you seemed tonight when you arrived with Phoebe.'

'You noticed that?' Ali frowned.

'I've noticed a lot of things about you.'

He was watching her intently and she felt a warmth flow through her veins. She was sitting close enough to him to see the gold flecks in his eyes, shimmering in the glow of the fire. She felt herself leaning towards him, ever so slightly, almost unconsciously. She was aware of others on the balcony, but they were hazy, blurred. Jake was the only person who seemed to be in sharp focus. She could feel him drawing her energy. Drawing her towards him.

But before she embarrassed herself, before

she ended up glued to his side, she remembered her experience with Adam.

Her experience with her ex had taught her she needed to practise caution. Adam had been smart, successful and attractive and he'd pursued her. She'd succumbed to him, fallen for his flattery. He'd made her feel validated—as a young, Indigenous woman it was something she'd craved at the time— but she should have been more cautious. She could be hot-headed and impetuous, but she needed to learn from her past mistakes.

She straightened up, putting some distance between them before she did something she might regret. Maybe their chemistry would prove too powerful to resist but now wasn't the time to find out.

'Yarran and Harper's story is a long one, but the abbreviated version is that I introduced Harper to Yarran and then she broke his heart.'

'They seem pretty happy though.'

'They are now. They've resolved their problems and are back together, but I felt like an idiot.'

'Why was that?'

'Harper was like a sister to me and when she broke Yarran's heart and ran off, she never said a word to me. Didn't say goodbye, just left, and I felt as if she'd dumped me too. As if our friendship meant nothing.'

'I take it that when you told me you had trust issues you weren't joking?'

'No, I wasn't. Not only because of Harper—my ex also did a number on me. I've forgiven Harper because I can see how happy Yarran is, but forgetting is proving to be a little harder and Harper and I are not as close as we used to be.'

She shivered as a chill ran down her spine. Despite Jake's jacket she was beginning to feel the cold as the temperature dropped.

'Would you like to go back inside?'

'Not really. I'm enjoying it out here.' She glanced at Jake's watch. It was later than she thought. They'd been sitting on the balcony for quite a while, ignoring everyone else at the party, she'd been lost in his company. 'But it's getting late. I should go home. I've had a hectic week.'

'Would you like a lift?'

'You drove?'

He nodded. 'I'm not a big drinker. I've got to take care of the one kidney I have. I don't want to make it work too hard.'

She wasn't a big drinker either. Years of being called out at any time of night to deliver babies meant she'd got into the habit of being careful. 'I'd love a lift,' she said as she gave him back his jacket. 'I'll get my coat and say goodbye to Ivy. I'll meet you at the lift?' She wasn't ready for anyone to see them leaving together. The hospital gossip mill would be running rife and she could do without that.

Jake was waiting for her with a smile on his face and she felt a thrill of anticipation as the lift chimed, announcing its arrival. He stretched his arm out, making sure the lift doors stayed open, letting Ali step in first. She draped her coat over one arm and pressed the button for the ground floor as he stepped in beside her. She brushed an errant strand of hair out of her eyes as she turned to face him and felt a tug on her ear as she tried to lower her hand.

'Hold on. Let me help you. You've got your bracelet tangled up with your earring,' Jake said. He stepped in closer, closing the distance between them. It hadn't been huge to begin with and she was pressed between Jake and the mirrored wall of the lift. He gently worked the charm bracelet free of her earring but didn't step back as the lift continued its descent. He was watching her with his dark eyes. Unblinking. Asking her a silent question.

Ali reached for him. Holding onto his jacket, she pulled him closer. She forgot about being cautious as she answered his question with her body.

He lifted her hand from his chest and kissed her fingers, slowly, deliberately, one by one, drawing out the moment of intimacy. Their faces were inches apart. He was watching her, studying her and then he moved another fraction closer, his head tipped slightly to one side. She tilted her face up to him and watched as he dipped his head, closing the gap between them. Only then did she close her eyes, waiting for the caress she was sure was coming.

Jake's lips brushed over hers, the gentlest of touches, so soft she wondered if it was nothing more than her imagination.

His mouth met hers again. His touch was firmer this time, more definite. Her lips parted and she tasted him. He tasted of champagne, bubbles and sunshine. She heard herself moan as his tongue explored her mouth. The outside world receded; it was condensed into this one spot, this one man.

Her heart raced in her chest and she could feel every beat as Jake's lips covered hers.

She closed her eyes, succumbing to his touch. His hand was on her bare arm, setting her skin on fire. She melted against him as her body responded to him. She was aware of nothing else except the sensation of being fully alive. She wanted for nothing except Jake.

She felt his hand move to her back. Her skin was bare between the straps of her dress, her shoulder blades exposed, and her flesh ached under his fingers. She felt her nipples harden as all of her senses came to life and a line of fire spread from her stomach to her groin. She deepened the kiss, losing herself in Jake before she remembered where they were.

Kissing in a public lift. Anyone could step in at any moment.

She pushed her hand against his chest, forcing him back, breaking the kiss.

'I shouldn't have done that,' Jake apologised.

Her heart was racing in her chest and her breaths were shallow. She could hear herself panting. 'It's okay. I wanted you to. I've wanted to know how that felt for a week. But not here.'

He took her hand as they exited the lift, holding it until they reached his car. He opened her door and she directed him to her apartment block and then to a visitor's park outside her building. 'Would you like to come up?' she asked.

'Are you sure?' he replied. They both knew where this was headed if he came inside with her.

Ali nodded. 'I'm forty years old. Divorced. No kids. I'm old enough to know what I'm doing.'

'I'm almost forty, divorced, no kids.' He grinned. 'I have no objections as long as you're sure.'

Alarm bells should have been ringing. He was not the demographic she'd told herself she wanted but the other voice in her head said—did it matter how old he was if it was just sex?

She decided to ignore the warnings. She was a grown-up. It didn't need to become a relationship.

Somehow they made it to her apartment without tearing each other's clothes off. She swiped her card and unlocked her door. He was right behind her, so close she could feel the heat radiating from him. She turned to face him and he claimed her lips with his mouth, kissing her swiftly and soundly.

His lips were soft but they weren't gentle. The kiss was hungry, intense and passionate. Ali had no time to think and Jake wasn't asking for permission. Not this time. He wasn't asking for anything. He was demanding a response. And Ali gave him one.

She kissed him back, unreservedly. Her hormones took control as blood rushed to her abdomen, flooding her groin and turning her legs to jelly. She knew she would have collapsed to the ground if she hadn't been in his embrace.

His hands were on her hips, holding her to him. Her hands were behind his head, keeping him with her. She walked backwards and he followed. His lips were on hers, his hands on her body, as she led him to her room. She didn't bother offering him something to drink or a tour of the apartment. Neither of them was pretending this was about anything more than desire, lust and longing.

She slid his jacket from his shoulders and then ran her hands under his shirt, trailing her fingernails lightly over his skin, and heard him moan. She grabbed the bottom of his shirt and pulled it over his head, exposing his flat, toned stomach. She dropped his shirt on the floor inside her bedroom door but as he started to undo his belt Ali stopped him.

'Let me,' she said. She undid his belt and snapped open the button on his jeans before sliding the zip down. She could feel the hard bulge of his erection pressing into her, straining to get free.

Jake stepped out of his shoes, not bothering to untie the laces, as she pushed his trousers to the floor. His jeans joined his shoes and shirt in an untidy heap. He was naked except for his underwear. Ali looked him over.

He was glorious. And he knew it.

He grinned at her and raised one eyebrow. In reply she put one hand on his smooth, broad chest and pushed him backwards until the bed bumped the backs of his knees and made him sit.

She stepped back from the bed. Out of his reach. He could watch but he couldn't touch. She wanted to tease him. She reached for the zip at the side of her dress and undid it slowly. She slipped one strap from her shoulder and then the other and let the dress fall to the floor. Jake's eyes were dark now, all traces of the gold flecks had vanished as he watched and waited for her.

She wasn't wearing a bra and she heard his short, sharp intake of breath as her dress dropped to the floor and she stood before him. She lifted her hands to remove her earrings but Jake held up a hand.

'Leave them in,' he said. 'You look sensational.'

CHAPTER SIX

JAKE'S VOICE WAS husky with desire. Lust coated his words, making them so heavy they barely made it past his lips.

Ali dropped her hands, leaving her earrings hanging from her lobes. She slid her underwear from her hips and went to him. She was completely naked but she didn't feel exposed. She felt powerful.

She stood before him and he reached for her, pulling her towards him, spinning her around and laying her on the bed. His thumb rested on her jaw. It was warm and soft, his pressure gentle. He ran his thumb along the line of her jaw and then his thumb was replaced by his lips. He kissed her neck, her collarbone and the hollow at the base of her throat where her collarbones met.

His fingers blazed a trail across her body that his mouth followed. Down from her throat to her sternum, over her breast to her nipple. His fingers flicked over the nipple, already peaked and hard. His mouth followed, covering it, sucking, licking and tasting. She reached for his underwear and pulled it from his body. His erection sprang free, pressing against her stomach.

His fingers were stroking the inside of her thigh. She parted her legs as his fingers slid inside her. His thumb rolled over her most sensitive spot, making her gasp. He kissed her breast, sucking at her nipple as his thumb teased her. She arched her back, pushing her hips and breasts towards him, wanting more, letting him take her to a peak of desire.

Still she wanted more. She needed more.

She rolled towards him and pushed him flat onto his back. She sat up and straddled his hips. His erection rose between them, trapped between their groins. Ali stretched across him, reaching for her bedside drawer, searching for a condom. Jake sat up and took her breast into his mouth once more. She closed her eyes as she gave herself up to the sensations shooting through her as his tongue flicked over her nipple. Every part of her responded to his touch. Her body came alive under his fingers and his lips and her skin burned where their bodies met.

She felt for the condom, finding it with her fingers. She picked it up and lifted herself clear of Jake, pulling her breast from his lips. Air flowed over her nipple, the cool temperature contrasting with the heat of his mouth. She opened the condom and rolled it onto him. Her fingers encircled his shaft as she smoothed out the sheath.

She put her hands either side of his head and kept her eyes on his face as she lifted herself up and took him inside her. His eyelids closed and she watched him breathe in deeply as they joined together.

She filled herself with his length before lifting her weight from him and letting him take control. His thumbs were on the front of her hips, his fingers behind her pelvis as he guided her up and down, matching her rhythm to his thrusts, each movement bringing her closer to climax.

She liked this position. She liked being able to watch him, she liked being able to see him getting closer and closer to release. His eyes were closed but his lips were parted, his breathing was rapid and shallow, his thrusts getting faster.

She spread her knees, letting him deeper inside her until she had taken all of him. Her body was flooded with heat. Every nerve ending was crying out for his touch. 'Now, Jake. Now.'

He opened his eyes and his gaze locked with hers as he took her to the top of the peak.

Her body started to quiver and she watched him as he too shuddered. He closed his eyes, threw his head back and thrust into her, claiming her as they climaxed together.

She collapsed onto him, their bodies slick with sweat, their skin warm and flushed from their effort. They were both panting as he wrapped his arms around her back, holding her to him. Content at last, she fell asleep to the sound of his heartbeat under her ear. To the feel of his lips pressed against her forehead.

'Good morning.'

Ali opened her eyes to find Jake watching her. They hadn't stopped to close the blinds last night and the sun was streaming through her windows. The light fell across Jake's naked shoulder, painting him with a golden glow. She smiled. 'Morning.'

'Did you sleep well?'

'Very,' she said as she arched her back,

stretching out her spine. The sheet fell from her chest and Jake leant towards her, kissing her first on the mouth and then her shoulder.

'I'd love to stay and pick up where we left off last night, but I need to get moving. But can I take you out to lunch later?'

'I wish I could, but I promised my sister I'd babysit for her. Marli is pregnant with number three and she's due in a couple of weeks so this is their last chance to have some childfree time before that one arrives. Can we go for brunch instead?'

Jake shook his head. 'I can't. Will and I are going to an open inspection this morning and I need to go home and shower first.'

'Will is house-hunting?'

'No, I am. I've been staying at Will's since I moved back from Melbourne three months ago and I think I'm about to officially outstay my welcome. It's time I found a place of my own.'

'You haven't looked to rent something?'

'I'm moving back permanently so I always intended to buy something.'

'You didn't like Melbourne?'

'I needed a change after my divorce. This job gave me a reason to come back.'

'Is your ex still in Melbourne?'

'No. She's American. She's gone back to the States.'

'Were you married for long?' Ali asked, amazed to find she knew so little about the man she'd just spent the night with. The man she'd just had amazing sex with. Should she know more? What did his history matter if it was just a sexual relationship? Would it be better to avoid learning too much about him? But, again, her curiosity had got the better of her.

'Ten years.'

'That's a long time.'

'It was. We were married much longer than we should have been, given the circumstances.'

'What do you mean?'

'We got married for all the wrong reasons. Chrissie's visa was expiring, we weren't ready to break up and I couldn't move to the US because I was still studying so we decided to get married. At the time I thought it was a solution to two problems—Chrissie could stay in Australia and I could escape from under the eyes of my watchful, nervous parents. My mother in particular was always risk averse because of my cancer and the ramifications of my surgery and I needed to get away. In hindsight, they weren't good reasons. It wasn't fair to Chrissie. What's that saying—act in haste, repent at leisure? We grew apart, or perhaps didn't have enough in common to begin with, and eventually I let her down. When she needed me, I wasn't there. But after the divorce I wanted a fresh start and my parents are getting older. I'm an only child. It's time to be a dutiful son, or at least to try to be one. But,' he concluded, obviously deciding that potted history was sufficient, 'back to my house-hunting. I need to get myself organised. Buying a house is another step on my new path. Why don't you come with me to see the house and, if we've got time, we can grab a coffee before you go to your sister's?'

Ali was tempted, keen to spend some time with him today, but before she could reply both their phones start beeping rapidly as multiple messages came through. She picked up her phone as Jake rummaged through his discarded clothes, looking for his.

Check your email.

Have you seen today's headlines?

Bosses aren't happy.

She showed Jake her messages.

'I've got similar,' he said, holding up his phone.

Ali opened the local news app to be greeted with the headline *CELEBRITY BABY CRISIS!*

The story was about Jasmine and Poppy, quoting a source that said the babies were critically ill and needed lifesaving surgery. There was no quote from Aaron or Emma and as far as Ali was aware they hadn't even issued a statement to say the twins had been born yet. But someone had announced the news, along with several inaccuracies.

Hospital staff were under strict instructions not to speak to the press and Ali knew most would never dream of breaking patient-doctor confidentiality. But someone had.

'That's not good,' she said as an email pinged into her inbox. She opened it to find a reminder to all staff to maintain privacy. And announcing that the leak would be investigated. 'I think I'll go into the hospital just to check on Emma. See how she's feeling,' she said, as she swung her legs over the edge of the bed and sat up. 'If you want to text me the details of the house inspection I'll see if I can meet you there.'

Ali turned up the music in her car and sang along as she drove down Glebe Point Road on her way to meet Jake. She flicked her indicator on and took a side street, turning down a familiar road. When Jake had texted the address to her, she'd looked twice. She couldn't believe the house he was interested in had been her granny's! She didn't believe in coincidences, she always thought things happened for a reason, but she wasn't able to work out what this turn of events meant. Not yet.

She drove past the house. There was an advertising board on the front fence with a flag saying 'open' sticking out of it. She found a parking space and walked back up the hill. From the outside it looked the same as it had when she'd last seen it ten years ago when her gran had moved out after her grandad had died.

It was a terraced house. A narrow, two-storey building with a wrought-iron front fence and a decorative veranda. She walked up the path and stepped through the front door, curious to see if the inside had been updated. There was a room to her right that had been styled as a sitting room with a small study nook in the corner. She ignored the stairs leading up to the bedrooms and bathroom that were on the first level and headed for the back of the house. The inside of the house had been painted, carpets had been pulled up and floorboards polished, but when the passage opened out into a kitchen and family room she could see that hadn't been touched since her grandparents had done a renovation thirty-odd years ago. The house was full of people as terrace houses in inner Sydney always attracted lots of interest and there was certainly scope for a buyer to put their own stamp on the place.

Through the kitchen window she could see Jake and Will at the back of the garden underneath the loquat tree. She was pleased to see the old tree; she would have been devastated if it had been removed.

She made her way through the garden, suddenly feeling a little awkward now that Will was there with Jake. Should she greet Jake with a kiss or not?

Before she could decide Jake took her hand and kissed her cheek and she noted that Will didn't seem surprised by either the kiss or her presence.

'How was Emma?' Jake asked.

'She's okay. The media were being kept at bay and Aaron is going to make a statement later. Poppy's condition is stable, she's no better but no worse, and Emma was feeling more positive about the mooted surgery,' she told him before asking, 'What do you think of the house?' She was curious to hear his opinion. She wondered if he was looking for a renovation project or if the dated fixtures would put him off.

'I really like it. It has a good energy. This is the third time I've looked at it. I think this house has a lot of potential,' he whispered, 'but I won't say that too loudly. Don't want to increase the competition.'

She smiled, pleased he liked it even though she was surprised he had his sights set on a three-bedroom house. This was why he was in the wrong demographic for her.

'Did you know you used to be able to see the water from up in the tree? And from the little balcony off the upstairs bedroom at the back. I wonder if you still can?'

'You can see the harbour from the bedroom, but I haven't climbed the tree. Yet.' He laughed. 'But how do you know that?

'This used to be my grandparents' house. My dad's parents,' she explained.

'Did you know it was on the market?'

'No.' She shook her head as she reached out a hand and stroked the trunk of the loquat tree.

'You wouldn't want to buy it?'

'I'm not really in a position to buy it. I've just bought an apartment.'

'You could sell that.'

'No. My apartment is all I need. It's safe, low maintenance, close to the hospital with good facilities. This house is far too big for me.'

'You could rent out a room.'

She shook her head. 'I'm too old for flatmates and I would rattle around in here by myself. The house needs a family. It needs conversation, laughter and love.'

Those alarm bells were ringing again. She'd have to make sure last night's activities were a one-off. She couldn't get involved with Jake. He had a lot of positive attributes, he was smart, considerate, handsome and good in bed, but he wasn't relationship material.

Ali had tried, and failed, not to check her phone constantly since the weekend. It was Tuesday and she hadn't seen Jake since she'd said goodbye at the open inspection and gone to Marli's. She hadn't bumped into him at work, hadn't heard from him aside from one brief text message. He seemed to have disappeared.

She pulled out her phone and reread his message from yesterday even though she knew it by heart now.

Thanks for a great weekend—catch up soon??

She'd replied.

Sure. Let me know what suits you.

But there had been no further contact.

She knew she shouldn't be bothered about that. It was probably for the best. He wasn't right for her anyway. He was looking at a family house. She should just let him go.

But her head and her heart were at odds. Or was it her head and her hormones?

Maybe all she needed was to find a replacement. Go on some dates and see what happened. Would she forget about him then? She wasn't sure it was going to be that easy to forget Jake Ryan.

Her phone beeped with a notification as she slid it back into her pocket.

Her pulse raced in anticipation as she pulled it out before disappointment sent her heart plummeting towards her stomach. It was a message from the girls' group chat.

Anyone free for lunch at Perc Up?

'Did you all have a good night?' Ivy asked as they sat down in their usual spot and waited for Harper.

'It was a fun party. Lucas's apartment is stunning,' Phoebe gushed.

'I can't believe you both left early.'

'I was tired,' Phoebe said.

Ali thought Phoebe still looked tired and was about to ask if she was okay, but Ivy hadn't paused for a breath. 'Ali, on the other hand, looked like she meant business. So spill, what happened with Jake? I noticed he left around the same time as you.'

'He offered to drop me home,' she replied, as there was no reason to pretend otherwise.

'You left with Jake?' Phoebe said, coming to life, just as Harper sat down.

Ali nodded as the spotlight was turned on her but made a mental note to check on Phoebe later.

'And…did you invite him in?'

'I did.'

'And?'

She could feel a smile spreading across her

face, she was powerless to stop it. Despite not having a follow-up planned, and the fact she'd been telling herself she was better off steering clear of him, that didn't erase the fact that Saturday night had been one very good night. 'He spent the night.'

'OMG, that was fast work. '

'I figured we're both consenting adults.'

'No judgement from me,' Ivy said, holding her hands up in mock surrender. 'Sex on the first date isn't taboo.'

'Well, I'm not sure it was technically a first date.'

'Okay, he didn't ask you out, but I did invite him to the party for your benefit.'

'That's not what I meant. I meant we'd seen each other before.'

'What? How come we didn't know that? When?' Ivy was full of questions.

'Technically that wasn't a date either, but we had spent time together before Saturday.'

'Doing what?'

'Rock climbing.'

'What?'

'It's a long story but I promised to accept a challenge, remember? That was it.'

'So are you a thing?'

'I have no idea.'

'And he's a rock climber?' Ivy asked. 'I didn't know that.'

'The charity fundraiser for childhood cancer that Aaron mentioned in his interview last night was all Jake's idea,' Harper said.

'What interview?'

'Aaron was on the news and current affair programme on his network last night, talking about the twins in response to the story in the media over the weekend, and he mentioned the fundraiser,' Harper said. 'You haven't seen it?'

'No.' All three girls shook their heads.

Harper pulled out her phone and searched Aaron's social media. She played the interview for the others when she found it.

'Some of you watching might know that my wife, Emma, was seriously injured in a fire a few months ago. She is recovering, but remains in hospital, and last week she gave birth to our twin daughters. They were born prematurely, and unfortunately Poppy needs heart surgery. We are lucky in Australia to have access to exceptional, mostly free medical care and, believe me, every day I thank the staff at Sydney Central for the care they've taken of my family.

'Poppy is not well, but her condition is stable. The doctors assure me that both my

daughters will be okay, but there are a lot of children in hospital with more serious medical conditions than my girls, including cancer. In two weeks' time there will be a fundraising event for a childhood cancer charity, with proceeds going towards programmes like Clown doctors, respite accommodation for country families and camps for children in remission.

'The event is an abseil at Circular Quay and the organisers are hoping to break the world record for the most people abseiling in a twelve-hour period. The record of 1372 people is currently held by Queensland and I think New South Wales can eclipse that. I'm taking part, and I'd like to invite any of you watching to take part too, if you feel brave enough. Or, if you can't physically participate, to make a donation to the campaign if you can afford to.

'The website details are running on the bottom of the screen and will be in my social media feeds too.'

'Wow! Well done, Aaron.'

'It was clever to mention that Queensland holds the record. There's always healthy interstate rivalry between us and Queensland.'

'Should we sign up?' Ivy asked.

'Yarran and I have signed up,' Harper said.

'I think we should do it,' Ivy said.

'I will if you will,' Ali said. She didn't feel as though she had a choice. Not after Aaron's plea and if her friends were getting involved.

'Has there been any more news on Poppy's surgery?' Harper asked Phoebe as Ali wondered if any of the others had noticed that Phoebe hadn't pledged to take part in the fundraiser.

'I've asked Zac Archer, the cardiac neonatal surgeon I met at the conference, if he would consult on Poppy's case. I'm waiting for him to get back to me but I'm hopeful he will agree to operate and then I'll be guided by him as to when it happens. I don't think she's strong enough yet to undergo surgery but he might think differently.'

Phoebe was having trouble maintaining eye contact with them while she outlined the plan and Ali's sixth sense was twitching. She knew there was something Phoebe was keeping from them.

Ali was lying on the couch in her apartment with her head in Jake's lap.

He'd gone looking for her today at the hospital, wanting to see her. He hadn't been able to stop thinking about her but work had been frantic for the past two days and he hadn't had a chance. She'd seemed a little reserved when he'd tracked her down and he was concerned she was having second thoughts about last Saturday night but when he'd invited her out for dinner she'd suggested a takeaway at her place. He was yet to determine if that was because she didn't want to be out in public with him or because she preferred the privacy of her own house.

He had stuff to sort out in his personal life—he definitely needed his own place to live and he still needed to settle into his role and mend his relationship with his parents—and he wasn't looking for a new relationship, but he hadn't been able to stop thinking about Ali. He didn't usually mix business with pleasure either. He'd met Chrissie through work…well, kind of. She was a sales representative with a medical supply firm so they hadn't actually worked together. But he didn't expect to do much work on the O & G ward. He could separate professional and private.

He looked around her apartment as he ran his fingers through her hair, massaging her scalp.

'What are you looking at?'

He looked down at her and smiled. 'Just getting a feel for you in your space. Will always says a home should reflect the person you are.'

'And what do you see?'

'Someone who values family.' Photos of her nieces and nephews were displayed around the room and drawings they'd done were stuck on her fridge. Her apartment was quite feminine to look at, decorated in soft colours, with plenty of plants and Indigenous artworks.

'How long have you lived here?'

'Almost four years.'

'You like living in an apartment?'

'I like some aspects of it. It suited me after my divorce. I wanted something close to the hospital, easy to look after but I'm starting to miss being able to feel the ground beneath my feet. House plants aren't really a good substitute for the earth. I feel a little disconnected, but I don't have time to garden. I don't need a house.'

'Four years is a long time to be single.' He was surprised that she was still alone. He knew family was important to her and she was gorgeous. He would have thought she would want a relationship. He thought someone would have swept her off her feet. He was certain many must have tried.

'Yeah. My marriage break-up was kind of rough. My ex did a number on me. He was another person in my life who betrayed my trust.'

He remembered her mentioning that at Ivy's party. He waited to see if she was going to elaborate.

'Adam was a lawyer, *is* a lawyer—I've got into the habit of talking about him in the past tense even though he's not dead, but he did kill our marriage,' she continued. 'We were both career-driven. I thought we had that in common. Obstetricians' hours are erratic, as you can imagine, especially before I became Head of Obstetrics and Gynaecology and still had a full patient list. He worked long hours too. When he said he was sleeping at the office because he was working on a difficult case, I didn't think anything of it. He'd done that before. But I came home one day and found him packing his bags. Turns out he'd been having an affair with one of his colleagues. He hadn't been staying at work— he'd been staying with her.

'I was blindsided and it's taken me a long time to get over. Not to get over him but over the way he treated me. The way he lied. But that's in the past now. I'm just glad the divorce was easy. There's no baggage. There's no reason to see him again. And no reason to talk about him either. So tell me, how many people have signed up now for your fundraiser? Aaron's interview must have helped your numbers?'

He noted her change of subject but he let it go.

'You saw that?'

'Harper showed me.'

'We had an additional two hundred people sign up today. I reckon Aaron's interview had a lot to do with that.'

'Do you know why he mentioned the fundraiser?'

'We spoke about it last week. I was talking to him about the event and he offered to promote it. As a favour. He wanted to give something back to the hospital. He was going to post something on social media, I wasn't expecting anything on the news channels, but he thought if he was giving an interview to set the record straight after that news report about Poppy's health then he'd add that in. All for a good cause is what he said. The fundraiser isn't really related to Poppy's condition but, as Aaron said, it's still for kids, many of whom are in more need of help than Poppy is.'

'Ivy and Harper have signed up for the fundraiser.'

'Not you?'

'I know I was keen to try abseiling, it looked like fun when we were indoors and when we were talking about a distance of ten metres, but I'm not so sure about doing it off a building that's over fifty metres high. The idea makes me nervous.'

'The hotel has been picked because of its location on Circular Quay. With the Harbour Bridge in the background, it makes for good publicity shots.'

'I'm not worried about the location. I'm worried about the height and the fixings.'

'There are secure bolts. There are permanent fixtures on the roof that are used for the window-washing platforms. Would you think about taking part if you had a chance to try abseiling beforehand?'

'Where? At the gym?'

'No. There's a come-and-try event this weekend in the Blue Mountains, near Katoomba. If you wanted to go, we could stay overnight.'

'You're suggesting we go away for the weekend?'

'Why not? I know we can do a day trip but it might be nice to spend the weekend together. Or Saturday night at least. Or have you already got plans?'

She shook her head.

'All right. I'll make the arrangements,' he said, noting to himself that, for the first time in over a year, he was excited about something.

CHAPTER SEVEN

'ALI, HAVE YOU got a minute? Ali?'

Ali looked up from her desk. She'd been lost in a world of daydreams. About Jake. For something that was supposed to be casual she spent a *lot* of time thinking about him. Today she'd been thinking about their upcoming overnight trip to the Blue Mountains, west of Sydney. This part of the world held a special place in her heart. It was her mother's country and, while she and her siblings had been born and raised on Gadigal land on Sydney's northern beaches, she still had an affinity with the Gundungurra people and their land. She loved spending time there, loved feeling connected to that country and she hoped she wasn't making a mistake by travelling there with Jake. She didn't want to make any memories that might be painful in the future. She didn't want to do anything that could possibly tarnish the love she felt for that country.

No. That was a ridiculous thought. An impossible outcome. She was attracted to Jake, that was certainly true, they had amazing chemistry, but no man was powerful enough to ruin her connection to country. The weekend would be fabulous.

Phoebe was hovering in her doorway and Ali turned her attention to her friend. 'Phoebe, hi! Sorry, what did you say?'

'I just wondered if you have a minute? I need to pick your brains about something.'

'Sure. Is it about Poppy? Is she okay?' Ali couldn't imagine why Phoebe would need her opinion on Poppy. After all, Phoebe was the neonatal surgeon and she'd already told Ali she was calling in an expert neonatal cardiologist.

'No. It's an O & G question.'

That made more sense. Phoebe was still hovering. She looked uncomfortable, which was confusing. 'Come in, sit down,' Ali said, trying to put her at ease. 'What's the problem?'

Phoebe sat but she didn't sit still. She slid her hands under her thighs and jiggled her legs up and down as she talked. 'I have a friend. She's just found out she's pregnant and she's got some concerns.'

'What sort of concerns?'

'It's a geriatric pregnancy and she's worried about all the things that could go wrong.'

'Do I know this friend?'

'I can't tell you.'

'Okay. How old is she?'

'Forty.' Anything over thirty-five was classed as a geriatric pregnancy. It seemed harsh but the statistics indicated an increase in problems after that age. Not for all mothers but certainly in enough that extra care was needed. Extra monitoring.

'Is it her first pregnancy?'

Phoebe nodded.

'And how many weeks is she?'

'About six, I think.'

'Do you know if the pregnancy was planned or not. Did she have IVF?'

'What difference does that make?' Phoebe asked.

A lot, in Ali's opinion. 'If she had IVF then she would have had more tests and more screening as part of the process. If the pregnancy was a surprise, then she might not have been taking folic acid or extra vitamins—' both of which could be important in older mothers '—and she might have been drinking alcohol, smoking… The incidence of pregnancy complications doubles in women in the thirty-five-to-forty age bracket when compared to those in their twenties. It's something to be aware of. Has her GP referred her to an obstetrician?'

'I don't think she's been to the GP yet.'

'Well, that should be her first priority. And then she should make sure she gets a referral to an obstetrician who is experienced in geriatric pregnancies. She should have more regular reviews and possibly some additional tests.'

'What sort of tests?'

'Some women want genetic counselling. Are there any issues on her side? On the father's side?'

'I don't know about the father's side. She hasn't told him yet.'

Phoebe looked worried and Ali got the impression she wasn't hearing the whole story. Then her mind started putting together the things Phoebe had and hadn't said. Phoebe's pale complexion, the fact she looked as if she'd lost weight, her recent behaviour—no coffee, not signing up for the fundraiser, and Ali couldn't recall her drinking any alcohol at Ivy's party.

Was Ali putting two and two together

and getting five? She wasn't sure but unless Phoebe confided in her it was all supposition on Ali's part. She'd have to take her word for it that she was asking for a friend. But her sixth sense was telling her something different.

'She knows who the father is though?'

Phoebe nodded. 'What would you do?'

'What are you asking? If you're asking if I'd go through with the pregnancy, you're asking the wrong person. You know I don't plan on having kids. Is your friend happy about the pregnancy? Does she want to go ahead with it?'

'She wants the baby.'

'In that case, I'd advise her to definitely tell the father asap. She needs to arm herself with the facts and get as much information as she can—about her family history and his. Then she can make decisions about what tests to have. If there's no reason to be concerned, then regular consults with an O & G will be fine.'

There were any number of things that could go wrong, especially in older mothers who were pregnant for the first time compared to younger mothers or older women who'd had previous pregnancies. Anything from gestational hypertension, gestational diabetes to abnormal placental positioning, increased incidence of C-section, miscarriages, premature births and babies with chromosomal disorders. Ali knew Phoebe would be well aware of this and could pass the information on to her 'friend', but she'd give her some reading in hard copy to look through later. Stress, rampaging hormones and fatigue did interfere with a woman's memory and sometimes her ability to absorb and retain information.

'I'll give you some information to pass on,' Ali said as she hit 'print' on her computer. 'Tell her there's no reason to be overly concerned. While there are things that can go wrong, older mothers often have been taking better care of themselves in their thirties than they were in their twenties. She'll probably have more resources than a younger mum, as statistics show older mums are also likely to be better educated and have a higher income, which will help the baby. Geriatric pregnancies, despite the unflattering term, are not uncommon. In fact, in the past twenty years the number of women giving birth in their forties has almost doubled.'

She handed Phoebe the info she had printed out. 'There you go. Give her this to read, then she can have the discussion about any further testing she might want. But remember, she doesn't *have* to do any of these. The choice is hers. Do you know if she's planning on going private or public for her doctor? I can give you a couple of names of obstetricians to pass on.'

'Um, public, I think. I'll have to find out.'

'Okay. Is there anything else I should know?'

Phoebe shook her head. But she didn't look any more at ease than she had when she'd walked into Ali's office.

'My advice for now would be, tell her to book in for an ultrasound in the next couple of weeks, certainly by eight weeks, just to check the development.' The first step was making sure it was a viable pregnancy.

'Okay.'

Were those tears in Phoebe's eyes? Ali knew something was definitely wrong and she could hazard a guess what it was but unless Phoebe was willing to confide in her there was little she could do.

Phoebe stood up; Ali stood too and wrapped her arms around her friend. Trying to convey in the gesture that she was there for her and would support her.

'And if you have any other questions, I'm here, okay? If your...friend needs a confidential ear or some non-judgemental advice, I'm right here.'

'You won't tell anyone about this conversation, will you?'

'Of course not,' she replied as Phoebe turned to leave.

For the first time in days, when Ali found herself alone with a quiet moment her thoughts were not focused on Jake.

She made a note to pay attention. To be there if Phoebe needed her.

Jake indicated and turned off the highway in Katoomba and then into the driveway of their hotel in the Blue Mountains. Sydney weather was mild, even winter could be sunny and pleasant, but today was not one of those days and it had been raining since they'd left the city and, while it had eased to a drizzle, the weather was still inclement. Wind blew the rain sideways and the abseiling had been cancelled, the weather conditions making it too hazardous. Ali had expected Jake to cancel their plans, but he'd insisted that the accommodation and dinner were still booked so there was no need to change all of their arrangements. She'd happily gone along with the new plan but she hadn't been expecting this level of luxury.

'Are we staying here?' she asked as Jake pulled up in front of a five-star hotel that she'd seen in passing but never visited.

'Yes. Is it okay?'

She laughed, delighted. 'It's gorgeous. I've always wanted to stay here.'

'Me too.'

She was pleased he hadn't been there before. Pleased it would be a new experience for them both with no memories of ex-husbands or wives.

'This is much fancier than what I'm used to up here,' she said after they had checked in. 'This is my mum's country. We used to come here a lot when we were younger but we'd always stay with family.'

'I didn't realise that. I thought you grew up on the North Shore.'

'I did. But Mum grew up here. It's my second home. My spiritual home in a way,' she said as Jake set their bags down to swipe the card that opened their room.

A canopied bed took up a large section of the room but large picture windows framed a view of the trees and the Jamison Valley and lent a feeling of spaciousness to the accommodation. In the en suite, the bath was positioned in front of a window to take in the same majestic view.

'This is incredible,' Ali said as she spun around to face Jake.

'I'm glad you like it.'

She walked over to the window and Jake joined her. Standing behind her, he wrapped his arms around her waist.

'What would you like to do first?' she asked, tipping her head to one side to look back at him. 'The bed looks comfortable.'

'It does. But the rain has stopped. Why don't we go for a walk while the weather is okay? Then we get to look forward to coming back here later.'

The rain had eased but low cloud still hung over the valley and Ali knew the break in the weather was likely to be short-lived. 'All right. Do you want to go to see the Three Sisters?'

The Three Sisters, massive sandstone rocks jutting out of the cliff, were one of the area's most popular sights but Ali hoped the rain might keep some of the crowds at bay.

They walked hand in hand from the hotel to the lookout. The air smelt strongly of eucalyptus and Ali knew it was the oil from the leaves that bathed the mountains in a blue haze and gave them their name.

Ali led Jake down to the Honeymoon

Bridge, which connected the cliff face to the Sisters.

'Do you know the story of the Three Sisters?' Ali asked as they stood underneath the first rock.

'No. Will you tell it to me?'

Information signs telling the dreamtime story were on display but because there were two versions of the ancient tale Ali was happy to give Jake her family's version.

'The Three Sisters are Meehni, Wimlah and Gunnedo and there are two stories about how they came to be here but because they are from the Gundungurra people—that's my mum's mob—that's the story we tell.

'The sisters lived in the Jamison Valley and when they were young they fell in love with three brothers from a neighbouring mob. The brothers wanted to marry them but marriage between the tribes was forbidden by law. The brothers refused to let that stop them and they kidnapped the three sisters. The brothers were warriors so they thought their plan was foolproof, but the kidnapping caused a tribal war. Now, Kuradjuri, a Gundungurra witch doctor, was worried about the three sisters so, in order to keep them safe, he cast a spell that turned them into stone.'

'Seems a bit harsh.'

Ali smiled. 'It would have been fine but, unfortunately, Kuradjuri was killed in the battle and no one else has ever been able to break the spell. So, here the Three Sisters sit, keeping watch for eternity over the Jamison Valley.'

'That story doesn't have a very happy ending.'

'Not yet. But there's still hope.' Ali laughed. 'It was one of our favourite stories growing up. We used to call the three sisters Alinta, Kirra and Marli, after ourselves, and we used to make our brothers and cousins fight pretend battles until we got tired of being stones and we'd join in.'

'There's five of you, right? And you all live in Sydney?'

Ali nodded. 'Yes. My parents, siblings, their partners, ten nieces and nephews, not counting the one Marli is expecting, grandmother and various aunties and uncles.'

'I can't imagine having such a big family. I'm lucky to have Will and his sister. They are like siblings to me but it's not quite the same thing.'

'We're lucky we all get along. Mostly.' Ali smiled. 'It's not always easy but even in our worst moments I never would have wanted to be an only child. I can't imagine it. Especially being a twin.'

'I'm not sure how I would have survived without Will. Because of my cancer diagnosis and treatment my parents were overprotective—which I get—but I often felt smothered and I think Will kept me sane. Spending time with him gave me the opportunity to live a normal life but it did drive a bit of a wedge between me and my parents.'

'How so?'

'Wrapping me in cotton wool just made me rebellious. As soon as I was old enough, I started pushing the boundaries, testing my physical limits, which in turn terrified my mother and led to lots of arguments. To escape all that I got married, moved to Melbourne then got divorced. In hindsight I probably shouldn't have used marriage as my escape route, but you live and learn. Other than my career I seem to be constantly disappointing my parents, which has strained our relationship. And my divorce certainly didn't help to repair the cracks in my relationship with them.'

'They didn't support you in that?'

'Not a hundred per cent. They're religious and, in their opinion, marriage is for life. They told me I should have tried harder to work things out but sometimes it's better to admit you've made a mistake and learn from it. Chrissie wasn't happy and I was making things worse. I'm hoping it's not too late to make amends with my parents at least. I've only got one family.'

He took her hand as they walked back across the bridge. The clouds had darkened and drizzle was falling again, making the walkway slippery underfoot. Jake looked up at the sky. 'I think the weather is about to put an end to our sightseeing. Can I interest you in high tea?'

'Is that what you call it?' Ali laughed and together they hurried back to the hotel, eager to get under cover before the heavens opened again.

The restaurant where high tea was served was beautiful. Large windows overlooked the valley, the tables were covered with crisp white tablecloths and sparkling chandeliers hung overhead. The table was set with bone china plates and teacups, polished silver cutlery and a vase of fresh flowers. Wait staff glided through the room delivering tiered silver cake stands to the diners.

Ali was glad she'd brushed her hair and applied some lipstick. After the walk they'd discarded their damp clothes, tried out the bed—it was as comfortable as it had looked—and then changed into fresh clothes for tea.

A menu listing dozens of different selections of tea, mineral waters and champagne was on the table and after the waitress took their order Ali looked around at the other guests and tried to guess what they were all doing there. What they were celebrating. There were a lot of couples, from honeymooners to retirees, and a larger group of women who she suspected were on a hen's weekend. She noticed a pregnant woman excuse herself from her partner and head for the bathroom. She had the gait of a woman in the very late stages of pregnancy and she looked quite uncomfortable.

The waitress brought their tea as a second waitress delivered their cake stand laden with Instagram-worthy afternoon-tea delicacies. Ali really wanted to start with a tiny lemon tart but she resisted the temptation—there'd be time for that later—and picked up a dainty cucumber sandwich instead. She'd finished the sandwich and a scone when she realised she hadn't seen the pregnant woman come back. Her seat at her table was empty and Ali's sixth sense started to buzz.

She picked up her handbag and stood up from the table. 'Can you excuse me?' she said to Jake. 'I'm just going to the bathroom.' She assumed the woman had gone to the loo. She'd quickly check on her.

Ali pushed open the bathroom door. The pregnant woman was leaning over the basin and gripping the edge so hard with both hands that her knuckles were white, and Ali could smell vomit.

She hurried across the room. 'Are you okay?'

The woman shook her head and started to cry. 'My water just broke and I can't move.' She stopped and gasped, her voice catching, and Ali suspected she was being gripped by a contraction. A strong one by all appearances. 'The pain is terrible.'

'Let me help you. I'm a doctor, an obstetrician actually.'

'Really?'

'Yes. I'm the Head of Obstetrics and Gynaecology at Sydney Central Hospital. Are you happy for me to help you?'

The woman nodded.

'Good. My name is Dr Edwards. But call me Ali.'

'I'm Olivia.'

'When is your due date?'

Olivia's baby bump was considerable. Ali wasn't worried about a premature birth, unless it was a multiple pregnancy.

'Ten days.' She broke off mid-sentence as another contraction took hold. They were less than a minute apart. This baby wasn't waiting for anyone. 'We're on our babymoon. My back has been achy all day, but I thought it was because of the different bed. I didn't think I was in labour.'

'This is your first baby?' Ali asked, thinking at the same time that Olivia had left the babymoon a bit late. With ten days to go anything could happen and, at the very least, by this stage in a pregnancy most women were getting fairly uncomfortable and the thing they needed most was a good night's sleep. But the excitement of a first pregnancy was real and the prospect of one last holiday was enticing.

'Yes.'

'It's just the one baby? You're not expecting twins?'

'Just...one,' she said as her breath caught again with another contraction.

'Let's get you into a different position,' Ali said. 'You might find kneeling on all fours more comfortable.'

There were only three cubicles in this

bathroom and none of them were occupied. Ali checked the entry door into the bathroom and was pleased to see it had a lock on it. 'I need to have a look at you to see what the situation is,' she said as she helped Olivia down to the floor. 'But first I'm going to lock the door so no one can come in unexpectedly.' Ali knelt beside Olivia. 'I'm just going to lift your skirt and remove your underwear, is that okay? I need to see what the baby is up to.'

Olivia nodded.

'Do you know if you're having a boy or a girl?' Ali asked in an attempt to distract her from the unusual situation they found themselves in. She didn't have a lot of time to build rapport or establish trust, she just had to hope Olivia was okay with this.

'A girl.'

'And where are you booked in for the delivery?'

'North Sydney.'

Ali had pulled Olivia's underwear down and she could see the baby's head crowning. That wasn't ideal.

'Okay, Olivia, I need you to focus on your breathing,' Ali instructed as yet another contraction gripped the expectant mother. 'Little pants, blow out through your mouth, you're doing well. Now, I've got good news and slightly less good news. I can see the baby's head, which means she's in the right position. But she's in a hurry. You're not going to make it to a hospital.'

'I'm going to have the baby here? In a hotel bathroom?'

'It looks like it,' she replied. 'So, this is what we're going to do.' Ali had heard the distress in Olivia's voice. That was to be expected but she needed to keep her as calm as possible. 'I have a friend in the restaurant, he's also a doctor. I'm going to call him and he'll fetch your partner. I saw you with him in the restaurant earlier. What's his name?'

'Jeremy.'

'Okay.'

Ali dug her phone out of her bag and called Jake. 'Hi, I've got a bit of a situation in the ladies' toilet. I'm with a lady by the name of Olivia, she's in labour and I can't move her. I need you to find her husband. They were having high tea. He's sitting by himself at a table behind you. His name is Jeremy. I need you to explain what's happened to him and bring him to the bathroom while I call an ambulance.'

Ali spoke slowly, giving Jake time to follow her instructions, waiting for any questions before she hung up and turned her attention back to Olivia.

'Olivia, Jeremy will be here in a moment. I'll call an ambulance now, but I will be here with you until they arrive. Have you had any complications during your pregnancy? High blood pressure? Gestational diabetes? Any issues?' She wanted to know if anything out of the ordinary had occurred, partly so she was prepared and also so she could forewarn the paramedics.

'No. Nothing.'

Ali dialled 000 and explained the situation, leaving her number with the dispatcher in case they needed her. Jake knocked on the door as Ali ended the call and she got up to let him in.

Jeremy rushed straight to Olivia's side while Ali spoke to Jake.

'I've called an ambulance, they're on the way. Can you notify the hotel about what's going on? They'll need to organise another bathroom for guests to use and direct the paramedics here when they arrive. Can you also see if the hotel has a first-aid kit and some towels or, better still, some large tarps or plastic sheeting as well?'

Ali introduced herself to Jeremy before directing him to sit in front of Olivia to help support her in kneeling. Fortunately, Jeremy seemed fairly level-headed even if he was obviously overwhelmed.

Ali washed her hands and willed Jake to hurry. The moment he returned, laden with towels and a first-aid kit, she resumed her position on the floor beside Olivia.

She was just in time. Olivia was fully dilated.

'Olivia,' she said, keeping her tone low and calm, 'you need to get ready to push.'

'I can't do it.'

'I know it hurts but you're almost there.'

'Hurts!' Olivia snapped. 'I've never had pain this bad. It's excruciating. Are you sure it's supposed to feel like this? I don't want to do this!'

'You're doing an amazing job. Stay strong. You can do this. Not much longer and you'll be holding your daughter.'

'It hurts so much,' she wailed.

'I know. But you can do this. Try to relax.'

'Relax! You're kidding me, aren't you? Have you had kids?'

Ali could feel her shoulders tense. She should be used to this question. Her patients regularly asked her this, but it usually came up during antenatal visits, never in the middle of a delivery. And she'd always had time to build rapport with her patients. Had time for them to realise that it didn't matter if she had children of her own. That not being a mother didn't impact her skills as an obstetrician.

She forced herself not to take Olivia's question personally. Olivia was in stage two of her labour—women always got cranky then. 'No,' she replied.

'Well, how do you know how I feel?'

Ali bit back the retort on her lips that wanted to ask if Olivia would expect a male obstetrician to know how labour felt, instead saying, 'I've delivered hundreds of babies, Olivia. I've seen all there is to see, and I've heard all the complaints, but trust me when I say it will all be worth it in the end.'

'Olivia, Dr Edwards is trying to help you,' Jeremy commented before Ali could tell him not to bother.

'Don't you start.' Olivia turned on Jeremy, lashing out in pain. 'It's your fault I'm in pain. I just want to go home. I should never have come on this babymoon.'

'It's okay, Jeremy.' Jake tried to appease the poor man. 'This is all normal behaviour. You'll both have forgotten it by tomorrow. Did they warn you about this in antenatal classes?'

Jake was right. It was quite normal behaviour but Ali wondered how he knew what was discussed in an antenatal class. But she filed that thought away for later—she had more important matters to deal with.

'All right, Olivia, squeeze Jeremy's hands and get ready to push with the next contraction. Ready…now!' she instructed.

The baby's head crowned and Ali guided it out, feeling for the cord, relived to find it all clear. She looked up at Jake to find him watching her closely. She nodded. *All good.*

'All right, Olivia,' she continued, 'have a rest for a moment. You're almost done. One more push with the next contraction.'

Ali rotated the baby's shoulders with the next contraction and caught her as she slid out. Jake handed her a clean towel and as she rubbed the baby's back the newborn began to cry. 'Good girl. That's the way. Congratulations, Mum and Dad, you have a perfect little girl.'

The baby's colour was good and she had a healthy set of lungs on her. Ali quickly checked the baby's reflexes and calculated her pulse rate before lying her on Olivia's chest and covering her with a towel to trap some heat.

'Do you have a name for her?' Ali asked as there was a knock on the bathroom door.

'Chloe,' Olivia said as the paramedics called out, announcing their arrival.

Jake let them in and Ali gave a brief handover before they assessed Olivia and transported her and the baby to hospital. Jeremy, who insisted he was okay to drive, followed the ambulance, leaving Jake and Ali alone in the bathroom.

There was a chair in the corner of the room and Ali collapsed onto it, surveying the mess.

'Did that really just happen?'

'It did. You were amazing.'

Jake was grinning and Ali found herself extraordinarily pleased with his compliment. 'Thank you. I'm just relieved it went well. I've never had to deliver a baby outside a hospital before.'

'That's even more impressive, then. She was lucky you were here. Jeremy should buy a lottery ticket on his way to the hospital.'

Ali laughed. 'Maybe he will. Did you get to finish afternoon tea?'

'No. I was waiting for you. Do you want to go back to our table?'

Ali shook her head. 'I think I need a shower.'

'Okay. Why don't I run you a bath and then I'll sort out what's left of the high tea?'

Ali was luxuriating in the bubble bath when Jake reappeared clutching a fresh bottle of champagne. 'Compliments of the hotel,' he said, 'and they've offered dinner on the house too, if you're up for it, but in the meantime they're going to bring the rest of our high tea to our room.'

He popped the champagne cork and poured her a glass. He handed it to her before answering a knock on the door. He returned pushing the room-service trolley laden with a three-tier cake stand, a fresh pot of tea and the vase of flowers.

Ali was starving and she lay in the bath drinking champagne while Jake passed her the tiny treats.

'Can I top up your champagne?' he asked as she finished her glass.

'No, I've had plenty. But I think I'll get out of the bath. I'm starting to go wrinkly. Would you pass me a towel, please?'

Jake plucked a towel from the rail and held out his hand to her. Ali reached up, putting her hand in his, and stepped out of the bath. Jake wrapped the towel around her and pulled her close.

'You smell so good.'

Ali slid the towel down from her shoulders, wrapping it around her chest and tucking one end into itself to hold it in place. She stood on tiptoes and kissed Jake's lips. 'Thank you.'

'Do you want to get dressed?' he asked.

She shook her head. 'Not at all. I want you to get *undressed*.'

'I like your idea better.' Jake grinned as Ali started to undo the buttons on his shirt.

CHAPTER EIGHT

JAKE PRESSED HIS lips to the side of her face, in front of her ear, before moving lower, dropping kisses along her jaw. With a flick of his fingers he undid the towel that Ali had just knotted around her chest, leaving her naked. His fingers grazed her breast and her nipple peaked. He bent his head and pressed his lips against the swell of her breast before running his tongue over her nipple and making Ali feel as if she could dissolve.

She put her index finger under his chin and lifted his head, bringing his lips back to hers. She slid her arms around his neck as she pressed herself against him. His tongue explored her mouth. Tasting. Teasing, deeper and harder this time. There was an urgency to their movements now.

She felt his hand trace over the curve of her hip. Her skin was on fire. A waterfall of heat and desire started in her belly, overflowed and ran through her like a river. She could feel the moisture pooling between her thighs and she tightened her arms around his neck, holding herself up as her legs threatened to give way.

Jake scooped her up and carried her into the bedroom, putting her down on the edge of the bed as he divested himself of all of his clothes.

Ali reached for him, admiring his naked form as she ran her hand along the length of his shaft. She felt him quiver as her fingers rolled across the tip, using the moisture she found there to decrease the friction and smooth her movements.

He leant forwards and ran his fingers up the inside of her right thigh. Ali closed her eyes and spread her legs for him. He slid his fingers inside her, making her gasp as he circled her most sensitive spot with his thumb. She moaned and arched her back.

He reached for the bedside table and handed her a condom. She tore the packet open and rolled it onto him. He was hard and hot under her palm; she was warm and wet to his touch. She arched her hips towards him She was ready now. She didn't want to wait. She couldn't wait.

She opened her legs and guided him into

her, welcoming the full length of him. She lifted her hips and let him fill her. He pushed against her and she met his thrusts, timing them with her own. They moved together, matching their rhythms as if they'd been doing this for ever.

Jake gathered her hands and held them above her head, stretching her out and exposing her breasts, and he bent his head to her nipple as he continued his thrusts. The energy they created pierced through her, flowing from his mouth, through her breast and into her groin where it gathered in a peak of pleasure building with intensity until she thought she would explode.

'Oh, yes, Jake, don't stop,' she begged.

His pace increased a fraction more and as she felt him start to shudder she released her hold as well. Their timing was exquisite, controlled by the energy that bound them together, and they cried out in unison, climaxing simultaneously, leaving them spent and sated.

'Do you mind if I check my phone?' Ali asked. 'It could be Marli.' She hated people answering their phones at dinner, but the notification sound alerted her to the fact that the message was on her family chat. 'After the day we've had, I don't want to find out she's gone into labour,' she said as she retrieved her phone after waiting for Jake's nod.

'Is everything okay?' Jake wanted to know. 'You're not going to disappear on me two meals in a row?'

Ali smiled. 'Everything's fine. It was just Kirra checking that I'm still calling in tomorrow.'

'Your regular family Sunday get-together?' She nodded.

'Kirra's the middle sister? With four kids?'

'You've got a good memory.'

'Yarran has one child, Kirra has four, Luka, three and Marli is about to have her third.' Jake checked off Ali's siblings and their offspring on his fingers. 'But, other than Yarran and Harper, I haven't got my head around their partners' or their kids' names yet. You've got a big family. You didn't want to add to the number?'

'No.' Ali had been waiting for this question. She'd learned it was always only a matter of time before she was quizzed on her desire—or lack thereof—for children. She looked Jake directly in the eye and said, 'Does that matter?' knowing his response would make or break their time together.

'Not to me. To be honest, I hadn't thought about it until today when Olivia asked if you had kids. Given your choice of career, I imagine most people assume you have kids and it made me wonder.'

'Do you think people ask that question of male obstetricians? Males in general?' She heard the abruptness in her tone but frustration made it difficult to soften it.

'I didn't mean to upset you,' Jake said.

Ali knew he was trying to placate her, but she wasn't about to be soothed. 'Are you constantly asked if you have kids? Or why not? Or when you're going to start a family?'

'Okay, I get your point. I don't get asked those questions often at all.' He reached across the table for her hand and Ali forced herself not to pull away in irritation. She knew that if she wanted to have more than a casual relationship with Jake, then they needed to have this conversation at some point. It might as well be now.

Ali sighed and slowly withdrew her hand. 'You haven't upset me. Not really. I know I get defensive when this topic is raised but I'm constantly being asked if I have kids. Or when I'm going to have a family. If I say I'm not going to have kids, they assume it's because I can't. It seems inconceivable to most people that a woman might be child-less by choice.'

'You don't want kids?'

'No. I never have. I've chosen not to and that's hard for lots of people to understand. I get judged a lot.'

Jake was nodding but Ali wasn't sure he really understood her meaning. Which was—was he going to judge her?

'Is it a problem for you?' she asked.

'It's your choice. Why would it be a prob-lem for me?' He sounded puzzled.

'Because I like you,' she said. She needed to be direct, she needed to make sure Jake understood her message. 'And I'd like to spend time with you but in case our rela-tionship develops into something more then I need to be clear about the fact that I don't want children.'

Did she want it to be a problem? Maybe she did. She liked him but she'd only in-tended on having a fling.

'Ali, it's fine. I haven't got plans to have kids. And I like you too. I enjoy your com-pany as well and I'm happy just to see what happens.'

'I get that. But it's easy for you to say you don't want kids now. It's all fine until the moment you decide that, actually, you do want a family.'

Was she trying to create drama? Was she wanting to drive a wedge between them? Ali knew it was different for men. There was no time limit for them on starting a family. And most didn't have a biological clock ticking away. They didn't need one when they could sire children at any age. She knew Jake could have fun with her and then move on and start a family later. It had happened to her before. 'I don't want to mislead you about where I stand and I don't want you to mislead me either.'

'I'm not misleading you.'

'You're looking to buy a family house.'

'It's just a house.'

'For a family.'

'That's what you see because it was a family house for you. That's your association with it. I see a good investment. It's in a good location and I can afford it because it needs updating. That's where the appeal is for me. I need somewhere to live. Look at me.' He spread his arms out wide. 'I'm thirty-eight years old and sleeping in my cousin's spare room. Even if I wanted kids, I'm hardly the type of responsible male a sensible woman would think makes good father material.'

Ali disagreed. He was gorgeous, kind and had a secure job. He would be at the top of many a woman's list. 'But what about when you have all those things? If we want this relationship to go any further, I need you to say you don't want kids full stop. Not tonight,' she hastened to add. 'I want you to think about it properly. I don't want a rushed decision. Words are easy to say. I need them to have consideration behind them.'

'What do you want me to do?'

'Think about it, seriously think about it. Do you have friends with kids? Have you ever looked at them and imagined what it would be like to raise a child of your own? How that would feel? How did you feel when you were in Theatre for Emma's delivery? When Jasmine and Poppy were born?'

'How do *you* feel when you deliver babies?' he replied, turning the tables on her. 'It doesn't make you second-guess yourself?'

Ali shook her head. 'It's a privilege to be part of that moment in people's lives but there's certainly no hole in my life waiting to be filled by my own offspring. I get my fix from my nieces and nephews. That's enough for me. I love them and they love me, but I couldn't give myself over one hundred per cent to a child. I'm not cut out for that.

And that's really what they need. At least initially.'

'All I can tell you is that I've never felt compelled to have a family,' he said. 'It's hard enough making a relationship work between two people. Throw kids into the mix and, from what I've seen, it just makes things even harder. If you ever want to see a reason why people shouldn't have kids, I'll introduce you to my father. I've been a continual source of disappointment for him.'

'I'm sure that's not true.'

'You can ask him yourself, if you like. My parents are celebrating their fortieth wedding anniversary next weekend with a big party. Come with me.'

'To the party?'

'Yes. You'd be doing me a huge favour.'

Ali shook her head. 'I don't want to meet your parents if this thing between us is only going to be short-lived. If you and I are not on the same page, if you want children, then this can't go any further. I really need you to think about my choice to not have children, to see if that's something you're prepared to sign up for. If not, there's no point continuing to see each other, let alone meet your parents.'

'You'd call it quits now?' he asked.

'I would. We have amazing sex, but I want more. I want a relationship. I'd like to see where you and I could go but I'm not prepared to invest my time and energy in something that can't last. I already lost my marriage over my decision not to have children.'

Jake frowned. 'I thought your ex had an affair?'

'He did. But he also got her pregnant. I don't know whether that was planned or not. He says it wasn't but, in the end, he chose her over me. The mother of his child.' Ali sighed. 'I didn't want kids, *we* didn't want kids, but all of a sudden he was leaving me for a woman who was having his baby. All of a sudden he'd decided he *did* want a family. He'd always said he was happy not to have children, that it didn't bother him, but, at the end of the day, he left me for a woman who gave him a child. But my biggest issue with all of this was the lies, the betrayal. I just wish he'd been honest with me. Not about having a family—I accept that he hadn't thought he wanted one until it was presented to him—but he could have been honest about not wanting to be with me. Why pretend? I was more upset about the affair, really. But the whole experience made me question a lot of things. My judgement mostly.'

'Would you have changed your mind if you'd known what he wanted?'

Ali shook her head. 'No. And that's what I'm trying to explain to you. I don't want a child and, given my age, even if I changed my mind, it's unlikely to happen. If you want children, a family, then I'm not the right person for you. I'd rather get that out in the open now, I'd rather not be discarded again because I don't want children. I'd rather leave now.'

Ali knew in her soul there was a real possibility that she could fall in love with Jake. There was a connection between them that she couldn't explain but it went deeper than amazing sex, much deeper, and she didn't want to end up with a broken heart.

Jake stopped outside the NICU on his way to see Emma and Aaron. He scanned the room through the glass window looking for Aaron. He couldn't see him, but Emma was sitting beside Poppy's crib holding Jasmine in her arms.

He knew the twins were making progress, gaining weight and getting stronger every day. Jasmine in particular was doing well, but they were still so tiny. He could empathise with Emma and Aaron. He realised how scared they must be, how worried they would be about their daughters, and he was glad he didn't have to go through that. Watching Emma with her babies gave him a little insight into how his parents must have felt when he was diagnosed with the Wilm's tumour. Watching Emma, he could understand his mother's protectiveness a little better.

He watched for a moment, thinking about Ali's question.

Did he want children?

He'd been giving it a lot of consideration over the past couple of days.

Chrissie had wanted children. He'd imagined that one day he'd be a father because that was what his wife wanted but he could still remember how he'd felt when Chrissie had fallen pregnant unexpectedly. How nervous he'd been. Scared. Worried about his own health. He only had one kidney—what if he had a young family and something went wrong with him? Where would that leave them?

He'd been terrified that they were doing the wrong thing. And he knew he hadn't supported Chrissie properly.

Why hadn't he told Ali everything that had gone wrong in his marriage?

He knew he'd kept quiet because he hadn't wanted to look like a failure.

When they'd lost the baby he hadn't known what to do. He'd never found the right words to say to Chrissie. And that frightened him. That someone had relied on him, and he'd let them down so badly. His guilt had consumed him, and he was disappointed in his behaviour. Disappointed in himself.

Ali had asked how he'd felt when Jasmine and Poppy were born. He couldn't recall feeling anything but relieved for Ali that the delivery hadn't had tragic consequences. It certainly hadn't raised any burning desire in him to have children of his own though. It was a terrifying prospect in some ways, to be solely responsible for another human life. He did that every day at work, but he knew what he was doing then. He'd studied for years to become an anaesthetist, no one taught parenting skills. He didn't want someone to be a hundred per cent reliant on him.

He could think of a lot of reasons not to have kids but couldn't think of many reasons why he should.

He scrubbed his hands and pushed open

the door to enter the NICU. If Aaron wasn't there, he'd leave a message with Emma.

'Emma, hi, how are you doing?'

'Good. Starting to go a little stir crazy but I escaped over the weekend. Aaron took me out for dinner. Just a quick one—I found even after getting sick of these four walls, I couldn't bear to be away from the girls for more than an hour.' She smiled.

This was what Ali was talking about, Jake thought. This all-consuming love and devotion parents had for their children. Obviously with the recent traumatic events in Emma's life she was even more emotionally tied to her children than usual and would find it hard to be apart from them, but could he imagine being like that? He didn't know the answer to that.

'And Aaron, how's he managing?' he asked.

'I think he feels a little useless. And I'm worried about what he's up to at home—he's been tinkering. He's not good with down-time.' She laughed. 'Would you mind holding Jasmine for a moment? I just want to check Poppy's chart.'

'Sure. You haven't popped home to see what Aaron's been doing?' he asked as Emma passed him the baby.

'No. Ignorance is bliss. I've got enough to worry about without adding his projects to my list. But luckily he's now back in pre-production for the next season of his show. That should keep him occupied until Poppy's surgery and until we can bring the girls home.'

'Has Poppy's surgery been scheduled?'

'Not yet. But she's gaining weight so that's good news. I'm hoping that she'll be strong enough for it some time in the next few weeks.'

'I'm sure you can't wait to get them home.'

'Sometimes yes. And sometimes no. It's a little bit frightening thinking of how I'm going to manage. I get lots of help in here. Everyone has been wonderful.'

'The place won't seem the same without you,' he said. 'Could you pass on a message to Aaron for me? Let him know we've got fourteen hundred participants registered for the charity event. His celebrity status has really helped the project and I really appreciate his time and effort.'

'That's fantastic,' Emma said as she held out her arms, ready to take Jasmine back. 'He's really looking forward to taking part.'

Jake heard the NICU door open as he turned to hand Jasmine back to her mum.

'Jake!'

He heard Ali's voice and spun around. He could see she was surprised to see him and realised she'd probably assumed he was Aaron as parents needed to don hospital scrubs to enter the NICU. Her gaze dropped to the baby in his arms and her expression clouded.

Her voice was tight as she said, 'I can see you're busy, Emma. I'll come back.'

'What's all that about?' Emma asked as Ali turned and fled.

'Not sure,' Jake replied, even though he knew exactly what was wrong. Ali was picturing him with a child of his own. Him holding a baby was the last thing he needed her to see. 'But I'm going to find out,' he said as he handed Jasmine back to Emma and hurried after Ali.

'Ali. Wait.'

She kept walking.

He knew she would have heard him. Was she going to pretend otherwise? She took two more steps before stopping and turning to face him.

She looked stricken and he could imagine what she was thinking. He reached for her, gently holding her forearm, wanting to make sure she didn't run away before listening to what he had to say.

'Emma asked me to hold Jasmine while she checked Poppy's chart. It's not something I'm in the habit of doing. It's not something I asked for. But I have been thinking about your question. A lot. And can I imagine teaching a child to surf, ride a bike, abseil? Yes, I can, but I don't imagine it has to be *my* child. And could I live without that? Definitely. I'm sure there are lots of rewarding moments being a parent but that doesn't mean life is unrewarding if you're not a parent. Through the charity I am already involved with other people's children—often—and that's really satisfying. I don't need children of my own to feel complete. I want to find love again, but the first step is finding the person I want to spend my life with. It doesn't start with children. Not for me.

'I enjoy your company,' he continued. 'You've told me you enjoy mine. Let's see where this takes us. We might be enough but if you're going to let your assumptions derail us there's not much I can do. I'm just asking for you to give me a chance to prove to you that I mean what I say. Don't give up on us yet. On me. Come with me to my parents' party on Saturday night. Please.'

CHAPTER NINE

'Jake, please can you try to relax? You're making me wonder what I'm getting myself into.'

Jake had been on edge since he'd arrived to pick her up for his parents' party and, as the Uber dropped them off at his family home, she worried that things were only going to get worse. He'd become more and more tense the closer they got to Double Bay.

'Sorry, you're right. It's just I always expect things to end in an argument.'

'Come on,' she said as she reached up to straighten his collar before kissing him soundly in an effort to distract him. 'I'm sure everything will be fine.' She didn't know what the future held for them, but she had chosen to give Jake a chance and if she could support him tonight she would. She didn't want him to feel alone. She wanted him to know he had someone in his corner.

They were greeted at the door by a hostess who took their coats and directed them to the rear of the house.

The house was large, too big for three people and definitely too big for a couple in Ali's opinion. The floors were parquetry, the furnishings antique and everywhere, on almost every horizontal surface, was a large floral arrangement in shades of red. Ali knew Jake's parents were celebrating their fortieth wedding anniversary and she could see they'd obviously gone with a ruby theme.

'Jake, darling, hello.' A glamorous dark-haired woman, dressed in red, was headed their way.

'Mother.' Jake bent down to kiss her and then she immediately turned her attention to Ali. Ali felt exposed under her striking blue gaze.

'You must be Alinta.' She held out her hand. 'Lovely to meet you. I'm Lara.'

'And I'm Howard, Jake's father,' said a man who, despite his height, had been two steps behind Lara. 'Welcome to our home.'

'Thank you,' Ali replied, a little flustered. From Jake's description of his relationship with his parents she'd expected them to be cool, emotionally distant, but they were warm and welcoming. 'Congratulations on your anniversary, such a big milestone. And the house looks spectacular, the decorations are amazing.'

'Chris organised it all for us. Have you met Jake's cousin, Will, and his partner?'

'I have.'

'Chris has a wonderful eye for setting a scene,' Lara said. 'They should be here soon.'

'Alinta, you work with Jake?' Howard asked.

'Yes, I'm an obstetrician at Sydney Central.' For some reason she felt it was important to make her job title clear.

'Ali is actually the head of Obstetrics and Gynaecology.'

'Really? That's impressive.' Howard sounded impressed but Ali didn't miss the sideways glance he gave his son. Had she heard something else underneath his compliment? Was it something in his tone that suggested he wondered what Jake had been doing with his time? Why *he* wasn't the head of a department. Was this what Jake had been talking about?

'Well, please, enjoy the evening,' Lara said as she put her hand on Howard's forearm and prepared to direct him elsewhere. 'Jake, you will make sure to say hello to our old friends, won't you?'

'Of course.'

Ali was grateful that Will and Chris were at the party too. Jake was expected to greet all of his parents' friends but Chris had rescued her from the introductions and whisked her onto the dance floor. But after several songs her feet were starting to complain about her high heels and she begged a break to get a drink.

Lara came over to them at the bar. She greeted Chris warmly and Ali recalled Jake's comment about how his parents reserved their judgement for him. 'Are you two enjoying yourselves?' she asked.

'It's a lovely party,' Ali said sincerely. She'd like to spend more time with Jake, but the food was delicious, the drinks plentiful and the music from the sixties and seventies ensured the dance floor was full.

'Chris, if you don't mind, I know Jake's godmother would love a dance with you,' Lara said.

'I think I'll have to start charging—do you think your friends will make a donation to Jake's charity every time I dance with them?'

'I'm sure they already have. They're always good supporters of a cause. I should know,' she said as she shooed him away. 'Jake gives so much of his time to that charity,' Lara said as Chris departed for the dance floor.

'Is that a good thing?' Ali asked.

'Yes. It's kept him busy after his marriage break-up. That was such a dreadful time; we were all so upset. But it's good to see him happy again. Making a fresh start,' she said as she looked appraisingly at Ali.

Ali didn't want her to jump to any conclusions about her relationship with Lara's son. 'He seems to be enjoying his job.'

'Yes, yes, that's wonderful but it's his personal life that he needs to work on. We'd really love to see him settled down again.' She was still looking closely at Ali, who began to feel more and more as if she was under inspection. 'Jake said you're the head of Obstetrics and Gynaecology? You seem young to have such a high level of responsibility.'

Was she fishing for information? Ali wished people would just ask direct questions. She was used to preconceived ideas based on her gender, looks and ethnicity. She hated trying to guess people's agendas.

'I'm forty years old,' she replied. There was no point pretending. She was older than

Jake and she had a more senior role in the hospital and she couldn't change either of those facts. Not right now.

'And single?'

'Divorced.'

'Do you have children?'

'No.'

She knew the assumption now would be that she couldn't have them. That something was wrong with her. Or that she'd missed her window of opportunity.

'That's a shame.'

'Is it?' She wondered what Lara would say if Ali announced she and Jake were just having sex and not interested in a long-term relationship.

'Yes. I was hoping Jake would find a partner who would give him children and you of all people would know how fertility declines with age.'

Lara certainly wasn't keeping her opinions to herself. It was clear she thought if Ali wasn't going to provide her with grandchildren, then what was the point?

Be careful what you wish for, Ali thought to herself. She'd wanted direct questions but Lara's comment had taken her by surprise and she stood, speechless, while Lara continued. 'Jake would be a good father. He should have kids. It was such a shame about Jake and Chrissie. They should have tried harder to make their marriage work. They should have tried for another baby.'

'Another baby?' Ali wasn't sure if she'd heard Lara correctly.

'Yes. He hasn't been the same since Chrissie's miscarriage. We were all devastated. He'd been so happy about the pregnancy, and I really thought another baby would bring them back together but instead, they got divorced.'

Ali could taste the champagne in the back of her throat and thought she might be about to be sick.

She stood still, dumbstruck, as her insides turned to ice. She had absolutely no idea what to say and was still standing, silent and chilled to the bone, when Howard came and escorted Lara onto the dance floor.

Ali wished the ground would swallow her up.

She put her glass down on the table, unable to take another sip, and headed for the terrace. It would be cold outside, but she needed some fresh air.

But before she could make it through the door, Jake intercepted her. 'Is everything okay? You look pale.'

She stopped in her tracks and turned to him. 'I'm not sure,' she said, her voice steely and cool. 'Why didn't you tell me that you and your ex had a miscarriage?'

Jake shrugged. 'Why would I? It's not important.'

'Not important! How can you say that?'

'I meant, I didn't think it was important to tell you about it. Plenty of couples suffer miscarriages.'

'Your mum said you were devastated. You told me you didn't want children. I thought you might have mentioned that you lost a baby.'

'It didn't seem like a baby. Chrissie didn't look pregnant. I hadn't felt the baby move. Neither of us had. I didn't feel like a father.'

'Were you excited?'

'No. I was terrified. I felt trapped. The pregnancy wasn't planned. That was when I realised that our marriage was crumbling, but how could I leave now? How could I walk away when she was pregnant? Then when Chrissie miscarried, I was worried that the miscarriage was my fault. Was there something wrong with me? Had the chemo done some damage that was unexpected?'

'You should have told me,'she said.

'I let Chrissie down. I didn't want you to think I was a failure as well.'

'I don't think you're a failure. I think you're a liar. And that's much worse,' she said as she stepped around him.

'Where are you going?'

'Home.'

'I'll take you.'

'No.' She shook her head. 'I need some time on my own. Time to think about what this all means.'

'It doesn't mean anything.'

'I disagree. This isn't like finding out you lied about which football team you support, or that you're a cat person not a dog person. You and your ex-wife were expecting a baby! You only just told me you don't want children. How do I believe anything you've told me?'

'You're blowing this out of proportion. I didn't lie to you.'

'Don't tell me what I should be thinking.' Ali was angry. Really angry.

'It doesn't change anything. It doesn't change the way I feel about you, and it shouldn't change the way you feel. *That's* what's important.'

'No. What's important is that we're honest with each other. And what I'm feeling right now is that I need some time on my own. I think it's better if we don't see each other any more,' she said as she walked past him and headed for the front door.

She collected her jacket and bag and kept on walking. Jake's parents would probably think her rude for not saying goodbye, for not thanking them for the party, but she didn't care. She couldn't face them. She couldn't face Chris and Will. She couldn't face anyone.

She was holding back tears as she fled. She was a foolish, foolish woman.

She should have listened to her head when she first met him. She knew Jake couldn't be the right person for her but her sixth sense had told her otherwise.

She'd been fooled. But not by him.

She'd fooled herself.

She'd rushed things, forgotten that he was supposed to just be good sex. She'd let herself get carried away. Let her heart carry her away. Let her think they could have a future. She'd let her hormones rule her head. She'd gone all in way too quickly and now she was paying the price.

'You've got to be fricking kidding me.' Jake clenched his fists and stared after Ali as she walked out of the door before turning on his heel and heading in his mother's direction. He was furious—with Lara, not with Ali—but before he reached his mother he was intercepted by his cousin.

'What's going on?' Will asked. 'Did Ali have an emergency? I've just seen her leave.'

'My bloody mother.' Jake could feel the steam coming out of his ears.

Will put a hand out and held Jake's arm. 'Don't make a scene,' he told him. 'You'll regret it later. Come outside and tell me what's going on.'

'Mum told Ali about Chrissie's miscarriage.'

'What do you mean, your mum told her? You hadn't?'

'No.'

'Why not?'

Jake shrugged. 'It wasn't relevant.'

'Except it would seem that it was. She looked upset.'

'Ali doesn't want kids. I told her that didn't matter to me, that I was happy not having kids. I want Ali in my life. I'd rather have her and I didn't think that the fact that I *could* have been a father, but wasn't, was at all relevant. But now she knows, and she thinks I was trying to hide something from her.'

'You were.'

'But not for the reasons she thinks. She accused me of lying to her. She thinks that because Chrissie had an unplanned pregnancy it means that I want children. That doesn't even make sense, but she wouldn't let me explain. She wouldn't let me take her home.'

'Having a go at your mum over it won't help. It won't make any difference now the truth is out there. You should have been honest with Ali in the first place. Then it wouldn't matter what your mum said.'

Jake knew Will was right. It wasn't his mum's fault.

He ran his fingers through his hair and groaned. He wanted to punch something, throw something... Both reactions were completely out of character for him, but he was so angry. Except now he realised he was angry with himself. 'How do I fix this?'

'I don't know. But you'll need to talk to her.'

'She doesn't want to see me.'

'She'll calm down.'

Jake shook his head. 'I'm not sure that she will.'

'You're not fifteen. If you're meant to be together, you'll find a way. Give her some time, and use that time to build a compelling argument—or, if you can't do that, a compelling apology.'

Ali peered through the peephole in her door on Sunday evening before she opened it. If it was Jake she was going to pretend she wasn't home. But it wasn't Jake.

'Harper, what are you doing here?'

'Your mum said you weren't feeling well. She made you some soup and I offered to drop it off.'

'I'm not sick. I don't need soup.' Ali looked past Harper. 'Where's Yarran?'

'He's on a night shift. It's just me.'

Ali waited for Harper to pass her the container of soup. She didn't want to grab it from her, but she did want her to leave. She wasn't in the mood for small talk.

But Harper apparently had other ideas. 'Can I come in?'

'I don't really feel like company.'

'If Yarran was here, you'd ask us in.'

'That's different.'

'Why?'

'He's my brother. He's family.'

'You used to say I was like a sister to you.'

'That was before.'

'We were best friends once and I'm going

to be family. You can't avoid me for ever. I'm not leaving until I know you're okay.'

'I'm not okay. I'm upset but I will be fine.'

'Do you want to tell me what's going on? Maybe I can help.'

'This isn't something you can help with. This is about something I've done. I've been an idiot.'

'Is it Jake?'

'Why do you say that?'

'I recognise the signs of heartbreak.'

'My heart isn't broken,' Ali lied. But wasn't that exactly how she felt? She'd been telling herself all day that she was going to be fine. That she couldn't possibly be this upset over a man she'd known for only a few weeks. 'It's my pride that's hurt. I've been a fool. I trusted Jake and he let me down.'

'What has he done?'

Ali had stepped back and Harper had followed her into the apartment. Harper closed the door behind her and put the soup on the bench and flicked the kettle on. Ali didn't object. What was the point? She didn't have the energy to argue with Harper. They'd have a cup of tea and then Harper could leave.

'You'd think I'd know better by now. I trusted him and he let me down. He lied to me.'

'Lied? About what?'

'He told me he didn't want children. That he didn't need children in his life. Yet his mother told me he was planning a family with his ex-wife, but she had a miscarriage.'

'What did he say about that?'

'That doesn't matter. Don't you see? He was going to have a family. His mother said he was happy about it. Maybe he doesn't want children right now but what if he changes his mind like Adam did? I don't want to find out in a year or two that he does want children. I don't want him to leave me too. It's better to end it now. I'm not going to see him again. We'd barely started a relationship. I just need a few days to move on.' But her heart was heavy. 'I'm obviously not a good judge of character. Adam let me down. You betrayed me. Now Jake has done the same thing.'

'Don't you think you're being a bit melodramatic?'

'No.'

'At the risk of destroying our fragile truce, I think there's something you need to hear. You've always been very quick to make decisions. And to judge others for their decisions. Not everyone is like you. Not everyone sees the world in black and white, wrong or right, like you do. There's no middle ground with you.'

'What do you mean?'

'Maybe Jake didn't want children but when his wife fell pregnant what was he supposed to do? Maybe he changed his mind. Maybe he didn't. Theory and reality are two different things. Maybe when he was confronted with the reality of being a parent, he decided it was something he wanted. But that doesn't mean he's not allowed to change his mind back again. Maybe he's decided he'd rather have you. I've seen the way he looks at you.'

'But what if he changes it again? Where will that leave me?'

'I think you need to ask him that. You can't decide for him. You did that for me.'

'When?'

'When you decided I was in the wrong when I left Yarran and moved to London.'

'Well, you—'

'No. I wasn't,' Harper cut in. 'I did what I had to do at the time. There are two sides to every story, but you heard Yarran's and judged me accordingly.'

'You never gave me your side,' Ali argued. 'You never said goodbye.'

'Because I knew you would take Yarran's

side so what was the point? In your mind, he would be right, and I would be wrong. It was all I could do to tell Yarran. I didn't have the energy to tell you as well.'

'It wasn't just Yarran that you hurt. You were my best friend and you left without a word.'

'I know. I'm sorry, I panicked. He's your twin, I didn't expect you to take my side, but I couldn't speak to you about how I was feeling. I knew I was breaking Yarran's heart and I couldn't stand to have you hate me as well. Your family is so close. I never knew anything like that when I was growing up and after the childhood I had I was terrified that I wouldn't be able to live up to your family's expectations. I had no idea how normal families functioned. I didn't think I'd be able to do it. I couldn't bear the thought of letting Yarran down. I thought I was making the right decision. But I never got over him. I never forgot him. I never stopped loving him. He's forgiven me—don't you think you should too?'

'I have forgiven you for that. I see how happy he is now. He's had more than his fair share of sadness, of love gone wrong with you and then Marnie, he deserves to be happy and I can see that he is happy with you. I've forgiven you for that but I can't forget how betrayed I felt when you left without saying goodbye.'

'I promise you this is it. I'm not going anywhere. When I came back for this job, I never thought I'd have another chance with Yarran, but I did. He's my other half. My one. My everything. He completes me. When you meet the one you're supposed to be with you'll know what I'm talking about. Learn from my experience. I've wasted years running away because I didn't think I deserved love. You have a chance at something beautiful with Jake. I've seen how he looks at you. Why are you prepared to believe his mother over him? Surely he knows himself best. Don't throw it away over a misunderstanding. What is your heart telling you? It's the only thing that can be trusted.'

Ali didn't want to trust her heart. Her heart could break. Her head wouldn't.

'Take it from me,' Harper said, 'you need to learn to compromise.'

'But that's the problem,' Ali said. 'There's no middle ground with kids. You either have them or you don't.'

Jake was glad to be on the night shift for the week. He'd spent a couple of days hoping

Ali would realise she was throwing away something special, but wishing for something wasn't going to make her see reason. He knew he needed to apologise if he was going to have any chance of salvaging the situation. But, as Will had said, his apology needed to be compelling. He'd listened to Ali when she'd told him about her issues with Harper and her ex-husband and he knew he'd only get one shot to make things right.

He'd come up with a plan but he needed time to put it into place. His days had been spent fine-tuning the abseiling event and hounding Will, who he'd coerced into helping him with his apology. He'd been pleased he'd had something to occupy his time and his mind during the day, but the nights were dragging.

He headed for the lift, relieved to finally have something to do. He'd been called to the fourth floor, to Obstetrics, and habit made him scan the corridor, looking for Ali. But it was almost midnight and she was nowhere to be seen.

His patient was a pregnant woman who had reportedly been in labour for fifteen hours and needed pain relief. The attending obstetrician, Melissa Merrigan, wanted her patient to rest—in her opinion it would be a while before she was ready to deliver.

Jake stopped at the nurses' station and picked up the patient file.

Marli Bowden; husband, Simon.

Marli was an unusual name. Ali's sister, Marli, was due any day and his gut told him this patient would be one and the same.

He knocked on the door and stepped into the room.

Ali was the first person he saw and his heart did a funny little flip before he remembered that she wasn't speaking to him. Before he registered that she did *not* look happy to see him.

Her saw her stiffen as he walked into the room and knew that getting her to forgive him wasn't going to be easy.

What was she doing there? She wasn't the attending obstetrician. She must be there for moral support. That was just his luck.

'Hello, Ali,' he said. He couldn't pretend she wasn't in the room.

'What are you doing here?' she asked, her expression steely.

'Melissa ordered an epidural. I'm the anaesthetist on call.'

'Right,' she said as she turned to her sister, 'I'll wait outside.'

Jake waited to see if she had anything more to say, if she had anything at all to say to him, but she simply walked past him and out of the door.

'Hi, Marli, Simon, I'm Dr Ryan,' he introduced himself to the two people who had stayed in the room.

'Ah, you're Jake.' It was clear from Marli's tone that she knew Jake had upset Ali. He wondered if everyone knew. 'She's really annoyed with you, isn't she?'

'Yep.'

'Would you like me to speak to her?' Marli offered.

'No, it's my mistake. I need to fix it.'

'Can I give you one word of advice, then? Ali has trust issues—unless you can regain her trust you've got your work cut out for you.'

'I know about her trust issues,' he replied.

But that was only one part of the problem. It had been his behaviour that had made the problem worse. He should have had full disclosure. Will was right about that. But Ali had jumped to conclusions. She'd put two and two together and got five. She'd assumed that because he hadn't mentioned Chrissie's miscarriage it meant that he ultimately wanted children. Which wasn't true.

Ultimately, he wanted Ali.

'I have a plan to fix things,' he told Marli, 'but if she can't bear to be in the same room as me then I'm not sure how I'm going to implement my plan. But you've got other things to focus on. Melissa said you're after an epidural. She wants to see if you can get a little rest before this baby arrives.'

'Yes. I thought baby number three would come quickly. It seems to have a different opinion from me.'

'It must be a girl,' Simon said. 'There are plenty of stubborn genes in the females in your family.'

'It'll definitely be a girl,' Marli said with a smile before she turned to Jake. 'We've got two already.' She turned back to Simon and said, 'I hope you weren't expecting a boy?'

'Not at all. I figured it would be another girl. The more the merrier, I say. I love my girls.'

Jake could see Simon's pride and love and for a split second he wondered if he would be as effusive if he were a father. He figured, of course he would. You'd have to love your kids, right?

But he could live without them. He was certain of that.

* * *

Ali was waiting in the corridor but she had her back to Marli's door and Jake knew she was planning on avoiding him.

'Ali, you can't avoid me for ever. You have to talk to me.'

'No, I don't.'

'We work together. You will need to talk to me.'

'When I need to talk to you in a professional capacity I will, but I don't need to otherwise. I want to believe you but I don't know if I can. I don't think I should trust you. I don't know if I should trust myself.'

'But you'd trust my mother over me? You're choosing to accept her version of my story.'

'She told me how happy you were to be having a baby. Why would she lie about that?'

'What was I supposed to tell her? That I was terrified? That I didn't love Chrissie enough? That when she miscarried I felt relief—then I felt guilty for feeling that way? I was a complete roller coaster of emotions and so was Chrissie for different reasons. I couldn't support her and that was the final nail in the coffin of our marriage.

'I learned at an early age to lock my feelings away. I saw how upset my mother got if I ever talked about being scared. I know she was frightened of losing me so I learned to shield her from my feelings. I haven't shared my feelings with my mother since I was four years old so I couldn't tell my parents how I felt. I couldn't tell them I was relieved. I couldn't tell them I didn't love Chrissie. I knew what they would think and I was tired of disappointing them. I can't help it if my mother projected her thoughts onto my feelings after the miscarriage. I can't help it if she got it all wrong. Ali, you have to believe me. I haven't lied to you.'

Jake held his breath, hoping Ali would hear him. Hoping she would listen. But she was shaking her head.

'I can't do this now,' she said. 'Marli needs me.'

She walked away, taking Jake's hopes with her.

'Uncle Yarran,' Ali said as her twin entered Marli's hospital room. 'Meet Willa,' she said as she handed Marli's sleeping daughter to her brother.

Yarran cradled his niece in his arms and smiled at her. 'Hello, gorgeous girl, you finally made it.'

Ali watched Yarran and Willa. Holding babies suited him. He was a brilliant dad to Jarrah and Ali hoped he would have more children with Harper.

'Congratulations, Marli.' Yarran bent over to give Marli a kiss, making sure he protected Willa. 'Did you want to grab a drink tonight, Simon, to wet your daughter's head?' he asked his brother-in-law.

'I can babysit the girls for you,' Ali offered, knowing Simon was responsible for looking after his older daughters, Tallulah and Jazz, while Marli was in hospital. 'I haven't got any plans.'

'You should have plans,' Marli admonished. 'Why haven't you sorted things out with Jake?'

'There's nothing to sort out.'

'You could have fooled me. If there's nothing to sort out why were you on edge last night? You could have cut the tension with a knife,' she replied.

'What do you mean?' Ali asked.

'You disappeared as soon as Jake arrived and you only came back after he'd left.'

'You didn't need me in here while he gave you an epidural,' Ali said as she felt Yarran watching her closely.

'You need to talk to him. Cool your hot

head and sort things out between you before the abseiling event on Saturday.'

'I'm not going abseiling,' Ali replied. She'd made the decision to pull out of the event last night. There was no way she could face Jake.

'Why not?'

'I'm too busy with work.' She gave the excuse she'd concocted.

'Rubbish,' Yarran said. 'Work hasn't changed in the past four days and Harper and Ivy aren't too busy. They've committed to it.'

'The cause will get my fundraising dollars even if I don't participate.'

'This isn't about time or fundraising,' Yarran said. 'This is about Jake.'

Ali looked at him, certain Harper must have told him what was going on. She hadn't specifically asked Harper to keep what happened between Ali and Jake confidential and so she should have expected her to tell Yarran. And she knew Yarran wasn't going to let this go.

'Don't be a coward,' he said.

'Kirra, Jack, Mum and Dad are taking all the older kids down to Circular Quay to watch. They're expecting to see you, Yarran and Harper all abseiling. Are you going to let them down too?' Marli added.

Ali thought she'd rather let them down than see Jake. That would be too painful.

'Our family are not quitters,' Yarran said, and Ali knew he was certain he'd had the last word. He was right. The Edwardses didn't give up.

CHAPTER TEN

SYDNEY HAD PUT on a perfect winter's day, calm and sunny with a forecast of twenty degrees Celsius, but Ali's mood didn't match the weather. Normally such a fine day would lift her spirits, but she couldn't shake her lethargy. She was not enthused about anything.

She found herself on tenterhooks whenever she was walking the corridors. Half hoping to bump into Jake, half terrified of seeing him. She didn't know how she would react if she saw him. She missed his company. Missed him. But she'd have to get over that. There was no going back.

She'd woken up this morning dreading the day, knowing it was almost inevitable that she'd see Jake, even if she might not have to speak to him. She'd given in to her family's pressure. Yarran was right. She wasn't a quitter. She was a mature, successful woman, she could behave like one and get through the day.

Ali had half hoped for bad weather, perhaps enough to cancel the abseiling event but she knew that wasn't in the spirit of the charity. With fourteen hundred people signed up for the event surely there would be enough participants to keep her separated from Jake, she thought as she, Yarran, Harper and Ivy made their way to the hotel at Circular Quay. Phoebe hadn't changed her mind, she wasn't participating, but she had donated to the charity and had promised to come down to support them.

An area in front of the hotel had been barricaded to separate the participants from members of the public—both those watching and others who were just passing by on their way to and from the ferry terminal and along the waterfront of the quay. Spectators had gathered at one end of the viewing area and Ali looked for her parents and the rest of her family, who were coming down to watch, even though she knew that they wouldn't be there yet. Check-in was almost an hour before their descent time—far too long for young children to stand and wait. They were most likely still on the other side of the harbour, waiting for the ferry.

Members of the media were positioned inside the barriers. Cameras were trained on the face of the hotel. Ali looked up to see a dozen figures, of varying shapes and sizes, abseiling down the hotel. As a couple reached the ground, journalists, trailed by their camera crew, approached requesting interviews. Ali wondered how long the media were planning on staying. The event was scheduled to go on for twelve hours—that would make for a long day.

Other participants, easily recognised by the bright yellow T-shirts they had been given with the charity name in large letters on the backs, were being directed to marshalling areas by the event organisers, who wore black versions of the same shirts.

Ali recognised one who was at the end of a rope, belaying a participant. She watched as a man made his final descent, both feet touching the ground, as Will high-fived him. She saw Will give some slack to the line before he said, 'Off belay,' and unclipped the man's harness. Ali leant over the barrier as the man headed back into the hotel and called out.

Will turned and jogged over to her, kissing her on the cheek. 'Hi, Ali, good to see you haven't changed your mind.'

Ali glanced up at the hotel. 'I have to admit I'm a little nervous looking at the height of the hotel.'

'You'll be fine. I promised to belay you—you'll be coming down in groups of ten, grab the eighth spot, that'll be me.'

Ali nodded and then hurried to catch up to Yarran, Harper and Ivy who were checking in before heading to the marshalling areas. They were assembled outside and then ushered into the hotel for a video and safety briefing. They stowed their belongings, got organised into groups of ten and were then escorted to the top floor of the hotel and up the stairs to the rooftop.

They emerged into the bright morning sunshine. People in yellow and black T-shirts were everywhere, dozens of them, but her gaze was drawn instantly to Jake. He had his back to her, but she picked him out immediately even though he was on the far side of the building.

She might not want to see him but the connection she felt was still there. It was going to take some time before she managed to put him out of her mind. To move on.

That was okay. She knew she'd get there. She didn't think she'd ever forget him, but she'd learn to live without him. It had only been a month—it was ridiculous to think she wouldn't be able to get over him. Wouldn't meet someone else.

So why did it feel as if this was it? As if she'd never find someone like him? As if she'd never find what Yarran had found with Harper, what her siblings, her parents, Ivy and Lucas had found? Life was unfair. Why did the person she'd fallen in love with have to be the one that she couldn't have—?

Oh, my God.

She was in love with him.

She stopped walking as the realisation hit her, and Ivy, who had followed her up to the roof, bumped into her back.

'Are you okay?' Ivy asked.

'No.' Ali was frozen in place.

'I'm sure it's perfectly safe. We'll be fine.'

But Ivy misunderstood Ali's hesitation. It wasn't a fear of heights that had stopped her in her tracks. It was her fear of being in love with Jake. Her fear of having to live her life without him.

She was in love with Jake.

She rolled the idea around in her head, wondering how she was going to deal with that, when Jake turned to look at her. He smiled and she almost burst into tears. He was everything she wanted. He was enough for her. More than enough. Even after such a short time she knew he was the one. And if she was truly honest with herself, she'd known in half that time. Why couldn't she be enough for him?

Why did she have to fall in love with someone whose dreams weren't compatible with hers? Why was she constantly drawn to the wrong men?

'Come on,' Ivy said, 'it's our turn.' She took Ali's hand and pulled her forward. The group in front of them had their harnesses on and were in the launch area, ready to go. Ali's group was next.

An event organiser positioned a harness on the ground and Ali stepped into it, relieved that Jake wasn't the one responsible for strapping her in. She didn't think she could stand to be so close to him, to have him touch her. Not now. She was feeling vulnerable, exposed and emotional. She needed to get herself under control.

She focused on recalling the video briefing, running through in her head the process of abseiling. But that didn't help. Jake had been the one who'd shown her how to do this. The whole experience was connected to Jake and her memories of him. She'd just have to get through the morning and then, somehow, find a way to deal with her feelings. With him.

She held her arms out as a second harness was slid around her shoulders, half listening as the straps were clipped together and the fastenings checked. The group in front of them were now stepping off the building, disappearing over the edge.

'All right, you can make your way to the launching area for a final check.'

Ali took a deep breath. It was her turn now.

Large, numbered squares had been painted along the edge of the roof, extending back several metres. A thick cable, hung with signs warning 'keep out', ran along the outer edge of the building, a couple of metres in from the drop-off to prevent anyone from getting too close until they were ready to abseil.

She could see metal frames bolted to the fixing points. The fixing points were permanent, strong enough to hold a platform and two men as the window cleaners' equipment was normally attached to these bolts. Jake had told her as much and it had also been in the safety briefing, a way to reassure the participants that everything was strong, secure and safe. Ali wasn't worried about the bolts but there were any number of other things that could fail—the rope, the harness…her courage.

She and Ivy followed Yarran and Harper to the far end of the roof, stepping carefully along a painted yellow line as directed by the instructors to make sure they didn't stray off course. Yarran and Harper took squares nine and ten, staying on the inside of a red rope that ran around the perimeter. Ali stepped ahead of Ivy to make sure she would get square number eight so Will could belay her as promised.

The event leaders were double-clipped onto safety wires, enabling them to move back and forward along the roof, unclipping one fastening at a time. There was one leader per participant and as Ali glanced to her left, she saw Jake unclip his tethering before re-clipping himself opposite her. She knew he was about to check her harness and attach her to the abseiling ropes. This was the scenario she had been dreading but there was nothing she could do about it now. She had nowhere to go. She was trapped between him and the edge of the building.

His black T-shirt moulded itself to his frame, sitting flat over his abdominals and hugging his deltoid and shoulder muscles.

He wore sunglasses so she couldn't see his eyes. But he could see hers. There was nothing for her to hide behind and she was afraid her emotions were on full display. Afraid her panic and longing, loneliness and regret were written all over her face.

'Hello, Ali.'

He stood directly in front of her as he checked her harness. His hands were at her waist, then at her shoulders, as he tugged on the straps and checked the carabiners.

Ali held her breath as her heart rate went crazy.

His touch felt intimate, a completely different sensation from how it had felt when the other instructor helped her.

Jake connected her ropes. She still hadn't said a word and if he noticed he didn't comment. 'You've got two harnesses, shoulders and hips, and two attachment points,' he said as his hands moved around her body. 'The shoulder harness is a back-up, you're nice and secure.' He was clipping her to the fixing point now, securing her to the roof before he unclipped one end of the red rope that had separated her from the edge of the building. 'All right, you can step through and stand with your feet on the marks,' he said.

Ali could see two feet stencilled at the

edge of the building. She stepped into square number eight, positioned between Ivy at number seven and Yarran at nine. The painted feet faced the centre of the roof, so now she was standing with her back to the edge of the building. She looked over her shoulder—it was a long way down.

Her nervousness kicked in again. She hadn't really been worried about the activity, she'd been more nervous about coming face to face with Jake, but now she could see the drop she could feel her heart pounding, sending adrenaline coursing through her system. It was not helped by the fact that Jake remained in her square. If she put out her hand, she'd be able to touch him.

Jake and the other organisers had two-way radios enabling them to communicate with the team on the ground. One by one they called out, 'On belay!'

'Belay on!' came the response from each belayer down below.

'All right. Take a step over the edge.'

Ali looked at Ivy on her left and then Yarran on her right, waiting to see which one of them was going to go first.

Yarran had a grin stretching across his face as he gave everyone a thumbs up and stepped over the edge. He was fearless but

Ali knew he'd done this manoeuvre plenty of times in his role with the fire department. His departure left Ali looking at Harper.

'Are we really doing this?' Harper asked. She looked nervous too, which cheered Ali up.

'I think so.'

'Ready?' Jake asked.

Ali nodded and took a step back, a few seconds after Ivy but slightly before Harper. She imagined she was in the climbing gym. If she didn't look down, she could pretend it was only ten metres to the ground and that there was a soft mat waiting at the bottom.

Yarran was already a few metres below them. He had his feet planted on the wall of the building and he was sitting back in his harness, relaxed, waiting for them all to step over.

Ali breathed out, exhaling audibly with relief as her harness held her weight.

They all began to walk down the wall, tentatively at first, one foot at a time, keeping their feet lined up with their hips. The ropes were holding and Ali let herself look down again.

Yarran was getting into the swing of the exercise—literally. She watched as he pushed off, swinging out into thin air, before coming back in, his feet wide, his knees flexed to absorb the impact as he landed back on the building back with a massive grin on his face. 'Come on, try it!' he encouraged.

Ivy gave a little push off the wall, not as powerful as Yarran's but enough to get her to swing out a little way before coming back to the wall. She repeated the move with a little more force and dropped several metres.

On her right Harper followed Ivy's lead. Not wanting to look tentative, Ali did the same, attempting a slight spring off the wall and back in. She breathed out—no disasters.

To her left she could see the Harbour Bridge, the sun on the water, ferries crisscrossing the bay leaving white water in their wake. She could hear the toot of the ferry horns, the sound of the traffic on the road to her right and the noise of the pedestrians and buskers milling around on Circular Quay below her. She was suspended above it all, but it didn't look too scary.

She did a second jump, no bigger than the first. She wasn't going to push hard. She didn't want to move too far from the wall— feeling as though she was within touching distance of the wall was somehow reassuring even though she knew the vertical surface was not going to offer any protection. She looked up to see she'd descended half a dozen floors but still had more than half the building to go.

Her gaze caught on Jake's gorgeous face peering over the edge, monitoring their progress. It was reassuring knowing he was there. It was a silly feeling—it wasn't as if he could do anything if something went awry and Will was the one controlling her descent.

Ali did a third jump and then a fourth. A little more forceful this time, a slightly bigger arc, a little longer spent curving out from the building, suspended in mid-air, her confidence growing. As her feet hit the building, she felt a jolt and her right hip dropped slightly. She looked at her right leg, wondering if she hadn't landed squarely but her feet were firmly on the building. She felt Will tighten the rope, taking the slack and holding her in position but she wasn't square on the building.

Her hips weren't level.

Her harness looked crooked and then she saw it. One of the carabiners had snapped.

She wasn't falling, she could feel that Will was holding her weight, but what happened next? What would happen if she kept descending?

She could feel panic rising in her chest. Her breathing was rapid, her heart was racing. She wanted to yell, wanted to tell someone that there was a problem, but she was frozen. Her throat felt tight, constricted. She couldn't force any words out and she wasn't sure who would hear her. Yarran, Ivy and Harper were all below her now and what could they do anyway? Yarran was the only one with any experience and he couldn't climb back up the building.

What was she supposed to do if there was a problem? She tried to recall the instructions from the safety briefing. She knew there was a signal. An arm signal. But she was holding tight to the rope with both hands and she was afraid to let go. She squeezed her eyes closed and pictured the briefing instructions. Arm out with elbow bent at ninety degrees indicated 'stop'. A straight arm, held out to the side, must mean 'there's a problem'.

She opened her eyes. Her chest was tight, her breathing shallow, she was feeling dizzy from a lack of oxygen. She forced herself to breathe, in and out, in and out, knowing she'd have to try a hand signal.

She tightened her grip on the rope with her left hand, just in case, and counted down from three in her head.

She loosened her grip on her right hand but couldn't make herself let go of the rope.

She thought she might be sick. She started to shake.

'Ali, is everything okay?'

She heard Jake's voice. She looked up and saw him give the 'OK' signal—the tips of his thumb and forefinger pressed together to form an 'O' shape.

She shook her head.

'What is it?'

She was too far away from him for him to see the problem and knew that her body would be blocking Will's view as well.

'A carabiner has snapped.' She finally found her voice but it sounded weak and she wasn't sure if it would have carried up to Jake.

'I'm coming down.'

She saw him press his earpiece firmly against his ear before he disappeared from view and Ali fought back a rising wave of panic. He'd said he was coming.

She saw his back at the edge of the roof. Saw him glance over his shoulder, heard him call, 'On belay.' She saw the rope that Yarran had used tighten as the belayer took up the slack. Yarran must have made it to the bottom of the building, but Ali was too frightened to look down. She didn't want to see how far she was. She was terrified of falling. Of plummeting to the ground.

She didn't want to die. Not on camera. Not in front of her family. And not without telling Jake how she felt.

Jake stepped over the edge.

He was by her side in two large jumps. His belayer holding him in position.

'Don't let me fall.' Her voice wobbled and tears sprang in her eyes.

He reached for her harness, grabbing onto it with one hand while he wrapped his other arm around her back, holding her to his side. 'You're not going to fall. I've got you.'

He let go of her harness and checked her equipment. 'We gave everyone more carabiners and ropes than they needed for safety. You're okay.'

'I'm afraid.'

'Ali, look at me. I won't ever let anything happen to you. I promise.'

He let go of her in order to take a spare carabiner off his own harness. He fastened it to hers, feeding the second rope through the loops, securing her again.

'All right,' he said. 'We've got to get to the bottom. Are you ready?'

'No.'

'You can do this,' he said. 'We'll walk

down the building, one step at a time. I'll be with you the whole way. Do you trust me?'

She did.

She nodded.

'Okay. Right foot first. Remember what I taught you. Step off, move your foot down, keep your steps small.'

He walked her down the wall, one foot at a time, until they reached the bottom. When her feet were on solid ground, he wrapped her in his arms.

'Are you okay?'

She was shaking but she was okay.

She nodded and fought back more tears only this time they were tears of relief. She wanted to bury her head into his chest. To never let him go.

'I need to talk to you,' she told him.

'I'm in the middle of the event. I can't leave now.'

'I know that, but I've got some things I want to say. Can you come to my house when you finish?'

He nodded and started to unclip her harness as reporters and cameramen approached them.

'I don't want to speak to the media,' she said. The only person she wanted to talk to was Jake.

'You don't have to. I'll make a statement.
Aaron is in the next group, so they'll be distracted by his descent soon enough. I'll tell
them it was a minor mishap, but the safety
measures held up. I don't want anyone to
panic,' he said as Yarran, Harper and Ivy
rushed over.

'Oh, my God, Ali, are you okay?' Ivy exclaimed.

'She's had a shock but she's fine. Can you
look after her? I can't leave.'

'Of course.'

'I'll see you at your place, but it could be
late,' Jake told her.

She didn't care. All she wanted now was to
be with him. It didn't matter when or where.

Jake's nerves were stretched tight. He'd had
to force himself to focus on the rest of the
event—it had been difficult to keep his mind
from wandering to Ali—and the adrenaline
surge had left him feeling wrung out. He was
relieved she was okay, that there hadn't been
a tragic turn of events, and was also relieved
that their safety protocols had been robust,
but he was concerned about how she was
coping. Was she replaying the incident in her
mind? Was she freaking out? Were Yarran
and Harper taking care of her? In hindsight,

would she blame him for the scare? After all, he'd been the one to check her equipment before the event.

Will had assured him it wasn't his fault. The equipment had been checked before use and then double-checked once each participant had been fitted out. It was an unfortunate accident but it hadn't been his mistake.

But that didn't stop the guilt.

For a moment today he'd briefly imagined a world without Ali in it. The consequences could have been far worse and he knew, without a doubt, that he wanted a life with her. Now he just needed to convince her that they were meant to be together.

He wanted to go to her the minute the event finished but a post-event gathering had been organised in the hotel bar and he knew he needed to stay for one drink with the charity committee, event organisers and volunteers, but his feet were itching to get to Ali.

On the television screen behind the bar the news was showing a clip of the day's events. There was an interview with Aaron and then a shot of Jake with Ali. They were standing together just after they'd reached the ground, she was wrapped in his arms and they were looking at each other as if there were no one else in the world. Anyone watching would see how they felt about each other and the picture gave him hope.

He needed to see her.

As the news story concluded he went to find Will and asked, 'Have you heard from Chris?'

He and Will had been working on a project that he hoped would win Ali over. After the incident he'd decided that he needed to implement the plan today. Will had done his part and then roped Chris in to set the final scene.

Will made a phone call. 'Everything is ready,' he said as he hung up.

'Thank you.' Jake hugged his cousin. He was grateful for his help and support and just hoped that their efforts weren't going to be in vain.

'Don't mention it. Just go and get your girl.'

CHAPTER ELEVEN

ALI OPENED HER door and stepped into Jake's embrace. He kissed the top of her head and then kissed her as she tipped her chin up and tilted her face to his.

His lips were soft and warm and her world settled around her again.

'How are you?' he asked as she took his hand and led him into her apartment.

'I'm fine. I feel embarrassed about over-reacting.'

'You didn't overreact.'

'I did a bit, but I was terrified. I'm okay now.'

'You're not furious with me?'

'With you? No. Why?'

'I checked your equipment.'

'It wasn't only you and, as you said, there was no way I could fall. Not unless all of the equipment failed. I freaked out but I really am okay now.' It was strange to find herself reassuring him, but it made her feel better to focus on his feelings. 'But the whole episode did make me realise a couple of things.'

'Like?'

She wrapped her arms around his shoulders and kissed him firmly. 'One, I don't think I'll ever put my hand up for abseiling again.'

'Fair enough,' he said with a smile.

'And two, there are some things I need to tell you.'

'I have some things to tell you too but there's something I want to show you first,' he replied. 'Will you come with me? We can talk once we get there.'

Ali frowned. She'd prepared herself to tell him how she felt the minute he arrived at her place and she didn't want to wait—worried that her courage might desert her—but she was curious to find out where he was taking her.

'Where are we going?' she asked as he unlocked his car.

'I have a surprise for you. A good one, I hope.'

He was quiet on the drive and his silence made her nervous. By the time he parked the car her stomach felt as if it were tied in a bundle of knots and it took her a minute to realise where they were.

He'd parked in front of her granny's old house and there was a 'Sold' sticker stuck to the advertising board.

'It's been sold,' she said. She could hear the disappointment in her voice, but she wasn't sure why she felt like that. It wasn't as if she'd been planning to buy it.

'Yes.' Jake opened the glove box and took out a key. 'It's been sold to me.'

'You bought it?' Her heart plummeted. She didn't want to hear that. Now she was glad she hadn't told him how she felt. This was a house for a family and she was convinced he only had bad news for her. She was convinced there would be no future for them. 'Why?'

'I needed somewhere to live.'

'But why this house?'

'What's wrong with this house?' he said as he got out of the car. 'I thought you'd be pleased it's gone to someone who appreciates it,' he continued as he opened the passenger door for her.

'It's a house for a family.' She looked at him, trying to read what was going on in his head but any sixth sense she had seemed to have deserted her. 'Is that what you want to tell me? That you want a family?' Thank God she hadn't embarrassed herself. Thank God she hadn't told him she loved him only to have it thrown back in her face.

'No, that's not why I brought you here. I told you I think this house is a good investment and it was also in my price range— those are the things that initially appealed to me. Will you come inside?' Jake held out his hand. 'I'll explain everything.'

Ali hesitated before placing her hand in his. She wasn't convinced it was a smart move to go with him. Was this a prelude to heartbreak?

But, once again, curiosity got the better of her and she got out of the car.

His hand was warm but it did little to dispel the icy chill that encased her heart. She let him lead her through the front gate. The porch light was on and Jake slipped the key into the lock, pushing the door open and bringing her across the threshold.

The house was empty. It had been staged for sale when she'd visited before, but the furniture had since been removed. Their footsteps bounced off the bare floorboards and echoed down the long hallway. Jake flicked on the lights and led her past the front room and the staircase into the kitchen and back living area.

The kitchen was stripped bare but there was a large roll of paper on the kitchen bench. Ali assumed it was paperwork from the sale and paid little attention to it until Jake let go of her hand and began to unroll the paper to reveal architectural drawings.

'This is what I wanted to show you. My ideas for the house. Will and I have been working on plans for restoration and updating—being mindful of its heritage. I'd like your opinion.'

'Why?'

'Because what you think matters to me,' he said as he put some weights on the corners of the plans. 'I want to open up the kitchen and living room and put bifold doors out into the garden. The front lounge will become a study and I'll put a powder room under the stairs and upgrade the bathroom on the first floor. I'll turn the smaller of the three bedrooms into a walk-in wardrobe for the primary bedroom and the other bedroom will be a study-cum-guest room. And out here,' he said as he picked up a remote, 'I'll put a new deck.' He hit a switch and the back garden lit up. Festoon lights hung in the loquat tree and hundreds of fairy lights flickered around the garden.

Ali gasped in delight. 'Were those lights always there?'

'No. Chris put them up for me.'

'When?'

'This afternoon while Will and I were wrapping things up at Circular Quay. He loves to set a scene.'

'It looks magical.' Ali walked over to the back window and gazed out.

Jake followed her and wrapped his arms around her waist. 'I thought I could hang a swing in the tree for you.'

'What do you mean, for me?' She spun around to face him, her brow furrowed in a frown.

'I needed to find somewhere to live and this house was a good option—it's in a great location and it has lots of potential, but the best thing about it is its connection to you. I felt it was meant to be,' he said. 'I bought this house for us.'

'For us?'

Jake nodded. 'I want you to move in with me.'

Ali was confused. 'But this house needs a family.'

'It will be a family house. We will fill it

with the family we already have. Your big one and my smaller one. That's enough.'

'You don't want children?'

'No.' He smiled. 'I don't want children. That's what I've been trying to tell you for days. I bought this house for you. For us. I want us to make a life together. Here. Just the two of us but sharing it with the people we love.'

'Is this going to be enough for you? Am *I* enough for you?'

Could she believe what she was hearing? She wanted to—her heart wanted to—but she was cautious.

'You are everything I need,' Jake told her. 'We have plenty of people in our lives. Your family, Will, Chris, our friends. There are plenty of people to share our love with, but I only want to give my heart to you. You are enough. You are all I need.'

'Are you sure?'

'I've never been more certain of anything in my life.'

'Just me? No children? Not now? Not ever?'

'If I'm going to be completely honest, I guess I always assumed I'd have children one day, but it wasn't a burning need in me. It wasn't something I had to do and, if I have to choose between having children or having you, I would choose you. Today, tomorrow, for ever. You are my future. You are all I need. All I want. We can make a life together and I know we can be happy. I love you, Ali.'

'You do?'

He nodded. 'I do. I've never felt like this before.'

'Not even when you got married the first time?'

'No.' He picked up her hand and kissed her fingers as they curled around his. 'Nothing like this. I felt guilty for so many things that happened in my marriage, but I don't regret that it ended. It taught me many lessons. Mainly that my relationship with Chrissie wasn't strong enough to begin with and definitely wasn't strong enough to withstand the challenges we'd faced.

'I could have had another baby with Chrissie if I wanted to keep her happy, but I realised I didn't. Having a baby wasn't the solution. I'd always thought people who imagined a baby would save a marriage were mad. When I realised that was how I was thinking—that our marriage needed saving—I took a step back and looked at my life. And I wasn't happy. We'd grown apart. So I chose not to have another baby and asked for a divorce instead. But I have no regrets. Everything I went through with Chrissie led me to you. We've both had failed marriages but that doesn't mean we don't try again. It just means we hadn't found the right person yet. And now I have. I've found you.'

'And what if we grow apart?'

'We're almost middle-aged,' he joked. 'We've had all our major growth spurts. I think we should now be pretty fully formed humans. Any growing I do from now on I want to do with you. I want to grow old with you. You are all I need. I have thought a lot about this, about you, about us, about what family means. I don't need children, I never have, but I do need you. We will be a family, you and me. I bought this house for the future, our future, the one I'm hoping to build with you. And, one day, if you do want to get married again, I'll propose to you under that tree. I need you in my life, Ali. I don't want to live without you. I love you.'

Ali wrapped her arms around Jake and rose up on her toes to kiss him. 'I love you too.'

'Thank God. I was beginning to worry.'

'I think I've loved you for weeks but, hanging from the side of the building today, I knew I had to tell you how I felt. I just hoped I wasn't going to die before I got the chance.'

'I was never going to let anything happen to you. I never will.'

Ali smiled. 'I figured, as long as I lived, what happened next didn't matter. If I survived it didn't matter if we ended up together or not. It only mattered that you knew how I felt. That I was honest with you. And honest with myself. Sometimes I feel like I loved you before I even met you, that you are part of me and I know you are supposed to be part of my life.'

'Is that a yes? You'll move in with me?'

Ali nodded. 'Yes.'

'Hold that thought,' he said as he let go of her and reached for a bottle of champagne that had been chilling, unnoticed by Ali, in the kitchen sink in a bed of ice.

'Let me guess—something else Chris prepared?' Ali said with a smile.

Jake nodded. 'Seems there are plenty of people who want us to live happily ever after,' he said as he popped the champagne cork and poured it into two glasses. He handed one to Ali. 'Here's to us and our future together.'

'To us,' she said as she touched her glass to his. 'I love you. Always.'

EPILOGUE

'HAPPY?' JAKE ASKED as he kissed Ali's forehead.

Ali nodded. 'Perfectly.' She smiled as she stood in the shade of the loquat tree and looked over the garden at their house. 'This is better than I could have ever imagined,' she said.

'You're pleased with the house?'

Ali turned to Jake and wrapped her arm around his waist. 'Not just the house.' She had a fabulous life with Jake. She was completely content. The renovations on the house were complete and Ali and Jake were hosting their first Edwards family Sunday barbecue. The house—*their* house—and backyard were filled with family and friends. 'I hadn't realised until today how much I wanted to be able to accommodate everyone in a home of my own,' she said as she rested her head on Jake's shoulder. After years of going to her parents' and siblings' houses on Sundays it was lovely to be able to reciprocate.

'I promised you we'd fill the house with our family and lots of love.'

'You did. It's wonderful. I love it. And I love you.' She lifted her head as Jake bent his head towards her, their lips meeting in a perfectly synchronised kiss.

'Hold that thought,' Jake said as Yarran called to him from the barbecue.

Ali let go of Jake and watched as he walked across the garden. Sometimes she still couldn't believe how well things had turned out. She felt as if she'd been waiting all of her life for Jake and now she had everything she'd ever wanted.

As Jake stepped up onto the deck Ali's attention was diverted by the arrival of Jake's mother, Lara. She was carrying Ali's niece, Willa, Marli's youngest daughter, who was now eight months old.

'Hello, Lara,' Ali greeted her, 'and hello, gorgeous girl,' she said to Willa, who was beaming at her aunt and holding her arms out to Ali.

Lara passed her over. 'She looks good with you,' Lara said as Ali took her niece and settled her on her hip.

Ali steeled herself, hoping Lara wouldn't

bring up the topic of grandchildren. She'd gone quiet on the subject recently—Ali suspected it was on Jake's instruction—and she hoped she wouldn't reignite the debate now that the house renovations were finished. 'Holding babies, delivering babies, is very different from raising babies,' Ali reminded her.

'I know. Don't worry,' Lara reassured her, 'I understand your position and I understand Jake's decision. It may have taken me a while to get my head around it but that was because of my own experiences and my own dreams.'

'What do you mean?'

'Howard and I tried for more children after Jake was born but it never happened. I put all my energy into Jake and when he was diagnosed with a Wilm's tumour I was so scared that I would lose him and that would be the end of my journey as a parent. The desire to have more children was something that never left me, and I felt guilty that I couldn't give Jake siblings. I wanted him to have more family and if he couldn't have siblings, I thought he should have children. I was putting my dreams onto Jake and that wasn't fair. All I really want is for Jake to be happy and I can see that he is. He has a family now, your family, and I wanted to thank you for letting me and Howard be a part of it too. I'm enjoying being a surrogate grandmother to your nieces and nephews.'

'That's enough for you?'

'It is. Jake's happiness and having a relationship with my son is more important to me than having grandchildren. The fact that we are re-establishing a relationship makes me happy and I think I have you to thank for that too.'

'You and I both want the same thing,' Ali said as Jake approached them. 'We both want Jake to be happy.'

Jake stopped at Ali's side and took her free hand. 'I need you to myself for a moment,' he said.

Lara took Willa off Ali's hip and carried her over to Marli, leaving Ali and Jake under the shade of the tree, giving them some space.

'If I could have everyone's attention for a few minutes.' Jake raised his voice, addressing their guests. 'Thank you all for coming here today to help celebrate the end result of our blood, sweat and tears. We want this house to welcome as many of you as often as you'd like to visit. It's a home for the generations. A home for love. Speaking of which, I think you all know how I feel about this gorgeous woman and I feel so lucky that she has chosen to make a life with me. Moving into this house is a big deal for us but I would like to acknowledge our commitment to each other in a different way.' He turned to face Ali. 'Ali, we have made a home together, but I'd like to commit to a life together. I love you and I promise to love you for the rest of my life. And now, with our family and friends as witnesses,' he said as he dropped to one knee, 'I'd like to ask you to be my wife. Will you marry me?'

Jake's proposal took Ali by surprise but in the best possible way. She looked at him, at his gorgeous face and beaming smile as he knelt before her, holding both of her hands. She heard the collective gasp of their guests and turned to them, looking at her parents, her siblings, Jake's parents, Harper, Ivy and Phoebe. Everyone was smiling but no one was smiling as much as Ali.

She looked back to Jake, who was still on one knee, waiting for her answer.

'I thought my life was complete since I met you. I thought I had everything I needed,' she told him. 'I didn't think I could want for anything more, but it turns out I want this. I love you, Jake Ryan, and yes, I will marry you.'

She didn't hear the cheers of their guests,

she forgot that her entire family and her friends were watching on, she only had eyes for Jake as he got to his feet and took her in his arms and sealed their promise with a kiss. For the moment, nothing existed except their love.

* * * * *